Damage

Debby Fowler

A Felicity Paradise crime novel

ISBN 978 185022 227 9

Published by Truran, Goonance, Water Lane, St Agnes,
Cornwall TR5 0RA
www.truranbooks.co.uk

Truran is an imprint of Truran Books Ltd

Text © Debby Fowler 2009
Cover photograph © Isabelle Corbett

www.felicityparadise.com

Acknowledgements
A special thank you, as always, to Jo Pearce who types
the final manuscript and has to cope with endless
alterations and frantic deadlines along the way. To Sally
Gilbert, faithful courier, to Robert Drummond Hay for
his knowledge of all things military and to Ivan and
Heather Corbett who make it all possible. A special
thank you to sons Dominic, Ben and Jake Pearce for a
spirited competition to be the one to choose the name
for Felicity's new puppy. Thanks boys – I hope you didn't
draw blood!

Printed and bound in Cornwall by R. Booth Ltd,
The Praze, Penryn, TR10 8AA

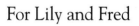

For Lily and Fred

PROLOGUE

June 1974, The Lizard, Cornwall

It didn't even make the national news, despite the public's normally insatiable desire for stories of death and destruction.

No one knew what caused the accident, or would ever do so. A naval helicopter taking off from Culdrose airbase climbed high and confidently into the sky. It was one of those perfect Cornish mornings when sky and sea competed with one another for first prize in blue perfection. Across Mount's Bay, the sea was shimmering like glass, stretching out towards the Scilly Isles. There was not a breath of wind.

Ten minutes later the helicopter fell out of the sky – mercifully, not on the busy little market town of Helston nor on any of the villages which pepper the Lizard peninsula. No, it crashed onto a dilapidated barn in the middle of a field, a good safe distance from the nearest farmhouse. The crew of two were killed instantly; the plume of thick black smoke from the burning fuel and straw could be seen for miles.

It was a tragedy, of course, but it could have been so much worse, some even described it as a lucky escape. Well yes, but not for everyone: not for the scrawny tortoiseshell cat who had just given birth in the warm straw to her first litter of four healthy babies; nor for her kittens, blind and still damp from birth but already suckling; nor for the little girl who tenderly, and with the natural skill of a farmer's child, had assisted at the birth; nor for her brother perched on a bale of straw at the very top of the barn, playing Batman rather than midwife.

For them it certainly was not a lucky escape.

1

May 2006, St Ives, Cornwall

Felicity Paradise was terrified. There was a small part of her brain which had not completely succumbed to nervous exhaustion and which told her that, having successfully raised two children of her own, cared for countless others and contributed to the raising of her grandsons, being left in sole charge of her five-week-old granddaughter should be something she took in her stride. The baby had been born ten days before her due date and still appeared so fragile and vulnerable, still had that strange look of wisdom and knowledge of the newborn ... and she was so very tiny. Felicity's daughter, Mel, and her husband Martin had named the child Araminta Helen, which had made Felicity wince, until they announced that she would be known as 'Minty'. Minty definitely suited her.

The carrycot stood on an old rug box close to the

open French windows leading from Felicity's sitting room onto a small balcony. It was an ideal spot – providing fresh air but warm and sheltered for one so small and new. Felicity stood at the end of the carrycot and for the hundredth time checked that Minty was still breathing: she was. Mel had been invited to attend a conference in Exeter. On the one hand she had been reluctant to leave her baby so soon, on the other she said it would be interesting to see if after the birth, she still had a brain, which she rather suspected she had not. She had expressed plenty of milk, and would only be away for about nine hours, six of which had already passed. She would be leaving Exeter to come home soon.

Outside there was the sudden and intrusive sound of sirens, police, a fire engine – Felicity couldn't tell. Hurriedly she shut the French windows, turning to peer at the baby who remained undisturbed. The sound echoed around the harbour, mercifully muffled now behind the closed windows. At the same moment the telephone rang. Darting across the room Felicity picked it up; again mercifully, the sound had no impact on the sleeping baby.

'Hello,' she said, breathlessly.

'Mum, it's me, Mel. Are you alright?'

'Yes, fine. Sorry, I was trying to pick up the phone before it woke Minty.'

'How is she?'

'She's fine too.'

'What did she think of the bottle, did she take it alright?'

'Perfect,' Felicity said. 'Both feeds; a model child and in between times all she has done is sleep.'

'I'm on my way now,' said Mel. 'I didn't stay till the end. It was very interesting though, I'm glad I went.'

'Good, well, drive carefully darling,' said Felicity. 'Don't rush, Minty's absolutely fine.' The joys of motherhood, Felicity thought, smiling as she replaced the telephone. Dear Mel – competent, independent, often stroppy and difficult and always opinionated – had been reduced in the first days of Minty's life to someone full of anxieties and a sense of inadequacy. No, not reduced – Felicity corrected her thoughts – she had been enhanced by it. The hardness in Mel that had made her successful in her career had softened, and that was no bad thing. Felicity wandered over to the window. Away across the harbour, close to the pier, a column of smoke rose into the clear blue sky. What on earth was going on? A chimney on fire perhaps. She turned away, dismissing the outside world, and looked again at her sleeping granddaughter, so tiny, so perfect and mercifully still breathing. She picked up a book and settled herself on the sofa to guard and to watch.

Felicity woke with a start to the sound of the doorbell below. Hers was an upside-down house – bedrooms on the ground floor, sitting room and kitchen upstairs. For a moment she was disorientated, then she remembered Minty. Jumping to her feet, she peered into the carrycot. The baby slept on, her tiny chest rising and falling reassuringly. The doorbell sounded again, the baby stirred slightly. Quickly Felicity hurried down the stairs and opened the front door.

Chief Inspector Keith Penrose stood resplendent on her doorstep in what appeared to be a new suit – charcoal grey with a tiny stripe – it looked good on him.

'Goodness, you do look smart,' said Felicity.

'Not before time,' Keith said. 'Most of my clothes are about twenty years old. The Super said I was starting to look like a tramp.'

'Well you certainly don't now,' said Felicity. 'Do come in, only be quiet. I've got a baby sleeping upstairs.'

'A baby,' said Keith. 'Whose baby?'

'Mine, well, not mine exactly, of course.'

Keith raised an eyebrow and smiled. 'You look wonderfully radiant and youthful, Mrs Paradise, but a baby would be something of a miracle child.'

'Enough cheek, Chief Inspector, come upstairs – quietly.'

They stood at the bottom of the carrycot admiring the baby who had slipped back into deep unconsciousness.

'She's a cracker,' said the Chief Inspector. 'What's her name?'

'Araminta,' said Felicity, cautiously.

'Blimey,' said Keith, 'that's a bit of a mouthful.'

'Only we call her Minty.'

'That's better, I can deal with Minty, proper job, it suits her.'

'I agree,' said Felicity. 'Tea, coffee?'

'Cup of tea would be great.' Hands in the pockets of his new suit, Keith wandered over to the French windows. 'I never tire of the wonderful view you have from here. You must have seen the smoke, of course.'

Felicity put the kettle on the Aga and turned to him. 'Yes I did, what's going on?'

'A fire, one of the cottages down Back Road West. It was really lucky the tide was in. The firefighters did a great job. They ran a hose into the harbour and put the fire out very quickly. A terrible mess, of course, but it's only the one house affected, the whole terrace could have gone up.'

'Why were you involved?' Felicity asked, crossing to join him by the window.

It was a wonderful spring day. Below them St Ives bay sparkled in the clear afternoon light. The town was still quiet, too early for any serious visitors. Felicity loved this time of year. Keith let out a sigh and turned to her.

'It's arson,' he said, gravely.

'Oh my goodness!' Felicity said. 'Really! Are you sure?'

'You must have read about the other attacks in *The Cornishman?*'

Felicity shook her head vaguely. 'I've been a bit involved,' she said, gesturing towards Minty, 'though now you mention it, I did see something on Spotlight, I think.'

'There have been a number of arson attacks in the area, a cottage just outside Nancledra, one up at Trencrom and another one at Gulval, all the Penzance side of St Ives but all relatively isolated cottages until now. Now we have one right in town.'

'And you're sure it's the same person burning these cottages? Has anyone been hurt?'

The Chief Inspector shook his head. 'No, no, it seems the arsonist is anxious not to hurt anyone. All the previous three cottages were empty and so was this one in St Ives. The trouble with this one, though, is it could have caused injury or even death to someone in an adjoining cottage. It's getting more serious, the arsonist is getting careless if he genuinely doesn't want to hurt anyone.'

'And how do you know it's the same person?'

'I don't have to be much of a detective for that,' Keith smiled, accepting a mug of tea and sitting down on the sofa. 'According to forensics, he just posts a package through the letterbox, paraffin-soaked rags wrapped round firelighters, sadly it's worked very well each time.'

Felicity collected her own mug and sat down on the chair opposite, frowning.

'And do you have a motive for these attacks?'

'The obvious motive would be some sort of pro-

Cornish anti-incomers movement. You may remember some years ago there were a number of cottages burnt down in Wales, as a protest against incomers. There are organisations here in Cornwall who want to keep Cornwall for the Cornish but I don't see them doing anything violent, not like this.'

'So do the cottages all belong to incomers?' Felicity asked.

'Yes, all of them.'

Felicity chewed on her lip, thoughtfully.

'It is a growing problem, Keith, this housing issue. My old friend Annie, you remember her – Annie Trethewey, she used to be my landlady before I bought this place?'

'Of course I remember Annie,' said Keith, smiling. 'Some character!'

'That's true,' Felicity said. 'Well, she has four children and nine grandchildren. Three of her children live in St Ives, but not her grandchildren, they'll never be able to afford to live in St Ives although they were born and bred in the town, as were their forebears going back generations. It's not right.'

'So given this is your sentiment,' said Keith, 'are you going to save me a lot of trouble by confessing to the arson attacks?'

'Afraid not,' said Felicity, 'I have a cast-iron alibi, Minty would be pleased to give you a statement to the effect that I have been here all afternoon. Seriously though, it can't have been easy, setting fire to a

9

cottage in the middle of St Ives in broad daylight.'

'The town is very quiet at the moment,' Keith said. 'No one saw a thing.'

'I read an article about arsonists not so long ago,' said Felicity.

Keith smiled at her. 'That was a funny subject to choose.'

'It was in a Sunday newspaper, I think. They say arsonists are usually loners, often people with severe emotional problems.'

'So I understand,' said Keith.

'I'm sorry,' Felicity said, 'of course, you'd know all about that sort of thing, being such an important policeman and all that.'

'And this important policeman had better get back to work,' said Keith, standing up. 'You're right though, arsonists very often suffer from some sort of condition like Asperger's, or have been the subject of some huge emotional trauma. The trouble is this has been going on for several weeks now, and we're no nearer knowing who could be responsible than we were after the first fire. With the season coming, we really need to get the villain caught and behind bars or it will start affecting visitor numbers.'

'Really?' said Felicity, surprised.

'Not yet – so far news of the fires hasn't gone beyond *The Times and Echo* and *The Cornishman*, but if a national were to pick it up, we'd be in dead trouble.'

'I'd have thought a few less visitors would make

your life a lot easier this summer,' Felicity suggested.

'I can't disagree with that,' Keith replied. 'I'm a Cornishman, remember, and I too, would like to keep Cornwall for the Cornish but even with our tourist industry, we're still one of the poorest regions in the whole of Europe and we just can't afford to have anything upset the visitor numbers. We've lost our tin mines, we've lost our china clay, our fishing industry, our flower industry and many of our farming activities – we've nothing left now but the visitors.'

'Food,' Felicity suggested. 'We have a growing reputation for food.'

'Only linked to the visitors,' Keith replied. 'Look, I'm not saying I like being part of one giant theme park, which is what we've more or less become, but there really isn't an alternative. My job is to look after them while they're here and to not let anything happen to put them off coming.'

'I just wish there was a way of keeping the visitor numbers up without destroying the heart of so many villages. Sorry, I'm on a bit of a soap box today.'

Keith had started down the stairs. 'How do you mean?' he asked, pausing.

'At least St Ives hasn't that problem – the Tate has made the town an all year round destination, but some villages are like ghost towns out of season, and as cottages get turned into holiday homes, first the school goes, then the shop, then the pub … it isn't right.'

'No, it isn't,' said Keith, reaching the bottom of

the stairs, 'but it's not a good enough reason for burning down cottages.'

'You don't know that is the reason.'

'No, I don't,' said Keith, opening the front door, 'that's the problem, I don't know anything at all.'

'No change there, then,' Felicity said grinning.

Keith smiled warmly in return. 'That's enough, Mrs Paradise.' He leaned forward and kissed her on the cheek. 'It's been good to see you. I wish we had more time to talk. I haven't even told you yet about the return of my wayward son.'

'No, you haven't,' said Felicity.

'He's left the Army and he's back with us and driving us nuts.'

'Let's have a lunch,' said Felicity, 'I'll come to Truro.'

'Good idea.' A thin high-pitched wail came from the room above.

'Sounds like Minty wants her granny,' Keith suggested.

Felicity watched affectionately as Keith set off down the lane leading to the harbour. For a man approaching sixty he exuded an extraordinary amount of energy and enthusiasm, but Felicity knew that for all his apparent laid-back good humour, his feelings ran very deep. Man's inhumanity to man troubled him a great deal; man's inhumanity to children was his particular horror. He paused at the turn of the lane and waved; she waved back.

It was a strange friendship, but one she

increasingly valued. She remembered the sensitivity with which he had unravelled the case and finally arrested the man who had been responsible for her husband's death. Ralph Smithson had never been prosecuted for that crime, there had not been enough evidence, but Inspector Penrose had got his man and he was now satisfactorily incarcerated in a South African jail for drug smuggling. It was a friendship that had blossomed during the four years that Felicity had now lived in Cornwall. She never regretted her move to St Ives and she had a wide circle of local friends. She couldn't walk down Fore Street without bumping into someone she knew, and she missed Oxford, her former home, hardly at all. But without the friendship of Keith Penrose, she wondered how well she would have settled. He was always there, steady as a rock, and she valued it enormously. Another wail sounded from upstairs. How could someone so very small make so much noise, Felicity wondered as she pounded up the stairs to the rescue.

2

'Any progress, Jack?' Keith looked up from the devastation which was his desk as Jack Curnow, his sergeant, came into the room.

'I'd like to offer you something, sir,' said Jack, 'but the truth is, I'm getting absolutely nowhere.'

Keith smiled appreciatively at his sergeant.

You knew where you were with Jack Curnow, he told it how it was, no messing.

'What we need,' said Jack, 'is CCTV cameras.'

'There are some in St Ives,' Keith said.

'Yes, but not near Back Road West which is probably why he chose the house, and certainly there's nothing out at the other cottages.'

'No,' Keith agreed, 'though there's probably the odd sheep or cow who could tell a tale or two.'

'Wouldn't stand up in court, boss,' said Jack. 'Actually I wasn't so much thinking of catching them in the act on camera, more of trying to find a vehicle in common. If I could have found the same vehicle in the four different locations on the right dates, I'd be getting somewhere.'

'You could try interviewing witnesses along the same lines, people often see more than they remember on first interview.'

'I've done that,' said Jack, patiently. 'No sightings at all.'

'Yet whoever did this must have used a car. Mrs Paradise thinks it's the work of a loner with problems, rather than any sort of political activist.'

Jack grinned. 'Oh, so you've been on a red-hot date with the lovely Felicity, have you, sir?'

'Mrs Paradise to you, and no, I haven't had a red-hot date, I just popped in to see her while I was in St Ives. That was her theory, for what it's worth, and as you know, she has an uncanny habit of being right.'

'I can't argue with that. So you're sure the cottage in St Ives was connected to the other attacks?'

'As absolutely certain as I can be until we have the forensic report,' said Keith. 'This time though the villain was lucky he didn't kill someone, the whole street could have gone up.'

'Could be a "her",' Jack said.

'Could be,' Keith conceded. 'But it's the male of the species who causes most of our problems, sadly.' He hesitated. 'Talking of which, have you seen anything of Billy since he got back?'

'Will,' Jack corrected. 'Your son now likes to be known as Will and yes I have, as a matter of fact. We had a pint the night before last.'

'How did you find him?' Keith asked.

'Angry, very angry about something. Have you got to the bottom of it, as to why he's left the Army?'

'No,' said Keith, 'he wouldn't talk about it, not to me, his mother or even his sister. Carly always used to be able to communicate with him, even when we couldn't.'

'I can understand him not talking to me,' said Jack, 'but I think he owes you and Mrs Penrose an explanation.'

'Me too,' said Keith, 'but every time we try to talk to him he simply storms out of the house like some ruddy teenager. He's twenty-seven now, he should know better.'

'You mean he should be a mature chap like me, sir?' Jack said with a smile.

'As a matter of fact,' said Keith, 'you're not far off the mark. I wouldn't mind at all if he was a bit more like you.'

'Can I take that as a compliment?'

'Just this once,' said Keith, grudgingly. 'Kids, who'd have them?'

'Don't say that. Our little Alice might not sleep at night but she loves her bottle and is always smiling.'

'You wait till she's sixteen,' said Keith, morosely.

At that precise moment, Keith's views on parenthood were not too dissimilar to Felicity's. Her daughter, Mel, had arrived breathless and excited at Jericho Cottage, Felicity's home, just as Felicity had rocked Minty off to sleep after her six o'clock feed.

'Tea or wine?' Felicity asked.

'Wine, oh better not, as I'm driving the baby. Tea please, Mum.'

'So what was it like, your conference?'

'Oh, it was great,' said Mel. 'It was so nice to see everyone again and to have a conversation about something other than nappies, feeding and burping. It was so stimulating.'

'What was the conference about?' Felicity asked, pouring the tea.

'Children in divorce,' said Mel. 'Made you think actually, about how easily people make the decision to have children, without thinking about the consequences if things go wrong, the consequences for the children, I mean.'

Felicity looked up sharply. 'There's nothing wrong with you and Martin, is there?'

'No, of course not,' said Mel, smiling at her. 'Relax Mum, nothing to worry about there, I promise. It's just parents are so self-centred, scrapping away about their own relationship and its problems, without so much as a thought for the children stuck in the middle of it all.'

'That's rather a generalisation, isn't it?' Felicity asked. 'In a lot of marriage break-ups, surely the children are the main consideration.'

'You'd be surprised how often they're not,' said Mel, looking down fondly at Minty who now lay angelically, arms above her head, sleeping peacefully. 'There's so much that needs doing; there's so much work on at the moment.' Mel glanced sideways at her mother. 'I really need to get back to work, Mum.'

Felicity set down her teacup. 'What, now?' she asked.

'As soon as possible,' said Mel. 'They really need me. The Truro office is up and running and there's just a stack of work coming in.'

'But Minty is so small, you can't go off and leave her. What would you do about childcare?'

'I was rather hoping you might do it,' Mel said. She ran her hands through her long fair hair, pushing the strands back from her face. It was a gesture from childhood when she was on the defensive but preparing to do battle.

Felicity stood up and walked over to the French windows. After a beautiful day, storm clouds apeared to be gathering on the horizon; the wind was getting up, the water in the harbour choppy and angry. Not a good omen, she thought.

'You mean, on a regular basis,?' she said, keeping her back to Mel, trying to adjust her thinking.

'They'd like me three days a week,' said Mel.

'What, the same three days every week?' Felicity asked, turning around.

'Mostly, depending of course on court time.'

'And what sort of hours would you be working?'

'It's difficult with the traffic getting into Truro in the morning and I'd need to be into work before nine, so I guess I'd probably need to leave about seven.'

'And home about twelve hours later, I imagine,' said Felicity.

'Yes, something like that.'

'And what were you thinking, dropping Minty off on the way?'

'I was rather hoping you might look after her in her home, it would be nicer for her.'

'And what does Martin think of all this?' Felicity asked, stalling for time.

'Actually, I haven't talked to him about it yet.'

'Well, don't you think you should before we discuss it any further?'

'No,' said Mel, 'Martin will go along with this. If he knows Minty is being looked after by you, he won't mind. It would be different if we were having to employ somebody who we didn't know, but we know Minty will be safe with you so he'll be fine about it. He always comes home for lunch anyway so he'll see her then and maybe you could cook him a bit of lunch. He's very fond of you, he'll enjoy having lunch with you.'

'Whoa, hang on a moment,' said Felicity. 'I haven't agreed to do this yet.'

Mel looked at her, genuinely puzzled. 'I thought you'd love it. Don't you want to see Minty and spend time with her?'

'Of course I do,' said Felicity, 'but I do have a life as well. You are asking me to give up nearly half the week to Minty's care and to spend it away from my home and my painting. I know you don't rate my painting much, but it does bring in quite a nice little income and I love it.'

'If money is a problem, of course I'll pay you to look after Minty.'

'That's not what I'm saying,' Felicity said, anger bubbling just below the surface. 'I have enough money to live on. What I am trying to say is, that in the last four years since your father died, I've built up a life for myself. It's not just my painting, I help out at the primary school one day a week, I have friends, I enjoy going into Truro for lunch or to the theatre. I know it probably all sounds deadly dull to you but after years of working and juggling my job around you children, I'm ready for this. It's a big commitment, three days a week.'

'Well, if you're not prepared to do it, I'll just have to find some paid childcare then, won't I?' said Mel, standing up and starting to collect her things.

'That's up to you and Martin, of course, but I'm not saying I won't do it,' said Felicity, 'I'm just saying I need to think about it.'

'Don't bother,' said Mel rudely. 'I don't want to put you out.'

'Oh stop it, Mel,' said Felicity. 'Just because you can't have your own way instantly, you're behaving like a petulant child. Just try and think about it from my point of view. I love Minty, I love you and I want to see lots of both of you. It's wonderful having you living in Hayle and being so near. I hope I can be a help to you and be a part of Minty's life as she grows up – picking her up from school, taking her to ballet classes and that sort of thing. However, if you are really going back to work so soon and you're asking me to look after her for three full days a week, twelve hours a day, I do need time to think about it. Also, having lived with your father for so many years, I know that nothing is straightforward when it comes to working in the law. Your three days a week will never work out quite like that, will it? You'll be ringing me up and asking me to come and babysit the day before a big case because you need to work on the brief, not to mention the cases which run over time. I just don't understand why you want to go back to work so soon. Minty is so small, you have your six months maternity leave – why not take it? Enjoy her, you'll never have this time over again, children grow up so quickly and you'll have missed out.'

'Oh Mum, for heaven's sake, I'll still be looking after her for four days a week, surely that's enough time for us to bond and for me to feel I'm still a proper mother. A lot of working mothers have to manage on a lot less time with their children.'

'I appreciate that,' said Felicity, 'and really it is none of my business but please think about it and talk to Martin before you make any rash decisions.'

Baby bits and pieces collected, Mel threw the bag over her shoulder. 'Well, I'll be off,' she said. 'It looks like I should assume you probably won't be helping us with the childcare.'

Felicity sighed. 'I can only repeat I didn't say

that, Mel. I said I needed to think about it and I don't think it is appropriate that you even talk it through with me until you've talked it through with Martin.'

'Dad would have wanted me to do this,' Mel said, her voice hard, her eyes threatening, knowing that she was treading on very dangerous ground and apparently not caring.

Felicity felt her stomach lurch. She put her hand on the kitchen chair to steady herself. She paused for a moment, eyes averted from Mel's challenging stare.

'I think you're wrong there,' she said after a moment. 'Your father had his faults, as you know, but he did love his children. I think he'd have had an absolute fit if I'd tried to go back to work when you were a few weeks old. It's the whole reason I took up teaching. It meant I was free in the holidays and at weekends and half term, all those times when you children needed me. My working day finished when your working day finished. I think Dad would have been appalled if you two had become latchkey children while I worked.'

'I'm not exactly suggesting Minty should be a latchkey child, am I?' Mel said, sarcastically.

'You know what I mean,' Felicity said.

'No, I don't actually, Mum. You and Dad always pushed me to pursue my career and now you're trying to stop me, just at a time when it is important I make my mark, if I want to get on.'

'I don't think Dad or I pushed you in your career, Mel. You were quite capable of pushing yourself. I've 'never known anybody as self-motivated as you.'

'Then recognise I need to do this, Mum.'

'Of course you need to do it, and of course you need a career. I'm just saying why the unholy rush? Enjoy these six months with your daughter and during the time you are at home, you, Martin and I can work out some sort of caring regime for when you do go back to work. You never know, Martin might like to take a day off work to spend with Minty?'

'He's self-employed, he can't do that.'

'I disagree. I'd have thought that was what made it possible. He could easily get someone to look after the Nursery for a day. He might love it.'

'I doubt it,' said Mel.

'OK, well maybe you're right, you know him better than me, of course. All I'm saying is we just need time to think it through, what's best for you and what's best for Minty.'

Mel started down the stairs, holding the carrycot in front of her. 'I wasn't expecting you to be this difficult, I thought you'd be supportive.'

'I am supportive, Mel,' Felicity said, wearily.

'You've got a funny way of showing it,' Mel called over her shoulder.

Felicity heard the door open and then shut none too quietly. I bet that woke the baby, she thought, and in the same moment realised that she had not even said goodbye to Minty.

Twenty-odd miles away, in a neglected cottage

23

on the outskirts of Mullion, a man sat in an ancient armchair in the gathering gloom in front of a single-bar electric fire. The fire stood in a very fine grate that would have played host to a splendid blaze, but the man had neither the energy nor the inclination to lay a real fire. At his feet, an old sheepdog lay, occasionally yelping in his sleep as he chased, and presumably caught, a number of rabbits which in real life he no longer had a chance of doing. On the arm of the chair stood a generous tumbler of whisky, on the sideboard, opposite where the man sat, was a photograph of a pretty little girl – a school photograph of her resplendent in neat pigtails and a school sweatshirt especially ironed for the occasion. The smile was open and friendly, brimming with confidence and pleasure in life. The man raised his whisky glass towards the photograph.

'Bless you, pet,' he said, and drank deeply.

3

'I've found the connection, sir.' Jack Curnow stood dishevelled, bleary-eyed but triumphant at the door of his chief's office.

Keith Penrose looked up and studied him closely.

'Have you been up all night, Jack?'

Jack's smile didn't waver. 'I'm used to it. That baby of ours is teething now and she wakes up all the time. We can't seem to do anything with her.'

'It passes,' said Keith, sagely. 'Just when you think you can't cope with another broken night, all of a sudden they turn civilized.'

'Can't come too soon for me, or Maggie, she's in pieces, poor girl. Anyway, the sleepless night paid off.'

'Go on,' said Keith.

'The common denominator between all four cottages is the Culdrose Air Base.'

'Really?' said Keith. 'Explain.'

'I got the clue right at the beginning, but just didn't make the connection.' said Jack. 'I spoke to the families at the Nancledra and Trencrom cottages. The

Nancledra lot live up in Derbyshire, the Trencrom family are from Reading but they are friends and have been for years because both men served as helicopter pilots at Culdrose. That's where they met when they were all on the Base together nearly thirty or more years ago now.'

'And the other cottages?' Keith asked.

'The one out at Gulval is owned by a chap called Jeffery Greenaway. He was a personnel officer working on the Base. He came out of the service about four years ago and now has a job in London, in an advertising agency, I understand. He bought the cottage in Gulval because he fell in love with Cornwall while he was stationed down here. He uses it as a holiday home and lets it for part of the year.'

Keith nodded.

'And the St Ives cottage?'

'The couple who own it come from Birmingham – their names are Brian and Elspeth Turner. Neither of them has ever worked at Culdrose but their son Gary does, he's been stationed there for a couple of years. He's their only child so they come down to St Ives quite a lot and take the opportunity to spend some time with him. He uses it when he has any leave, as a bit of a love nest, I suspect. They do let the cottage but only occasionally.'

Keith leaned back in his chair. 'Well, this all seems very positive, Jack, though at the risk of sounding a killjoy, it has to be said that an awful lot of families in this part of the world have connections with Culdrose.'

'But this is surely too much of a coincidence?' Jack looked momentarily deflated.

Keith smiled at him. 'I tend to agree with you. If the fires had all happened in Helston then the Culdrose connection would have been less surprising since so many families are billeted there. However, as the cottages are round St Ives, it looks like something more than coincidence.'

'I agree,' said Jack, obviously relieved that his hard work was not in vain.

'Tell me Jack, you're a local boy from the Lizard. How do the locals feel about Culdrose?'

Jack considered the question. He was exhausted and would have valued the opportunity to sit down but every available space, including the two visitors' chairs, was covered in Keith's paperwork. He leant against the doorway instead.

'I think everybody feels pretty positive about Culdrose,' he said. 'The Base provides a lot of work for non-service personnel as well as those in the Navy. It boosts the trade locally in restaurants, pubs and shops, and they rent a lot of houses locally. Generally, the Base contributes enormously to the economy of the area. They've been there a while too, it's not like it's something new, it's part of the landscape, part of the area and of course nobody underestimates the importance of air-sea rescue.'

'No, that's right,' said Keith. 'On this narrow strip of land surrounded by sea, without the helicopters from RNAS Culdrose, we'd be in a right mess.'

He stood up and began pacing the space between his desk and the window, always a necessity when thinking.

'So while there is resentment locally about incomers buying up cottages, inflating the prices, and then not living in them all the year round, if anything a property owned by someone connected with Culdrose would be more likely to be exempt from that kind of resentment. Do you think that's so, Jack?'

Jack nodded. 'Probably, boss.'

'In which case,' said Keith, 'whoever fired these cottages has a particular grudge against the Base itself. I take it that all four families don't know one another?'

'No, I checked that out,' said Jack, 'it's only the two at Nancledra and Trencrom.' He consulted his notebook. 'The Nancledra people are Edward and Moira Stephenson, at Trencrom the lady is a widow, a Mary Knightly, whose husband James was a helicopter pilot. She is particularly upset, she lost all the memorabilia of their marriage, a lot of photographs and keepsakes. She also fancies herself as something of an artist. She had all her work at the cottage because she was preparing for an exhibition in Newlyn and she's lost the lot. Her husband has only been dead about nine months. It's not been a good year for her.'

'I should say not,' said Keith, 'poor woman.' He

reached for his jacket from the back of the chair. 'OK,' he said, 'you know what happens next. You start searching for an incident involving Culdrose which might have caused some resentment locally. Be prepared to go back more than thirty years, people with a grudge have long memories.'

'Right,' said Jack, with a sigh. 'And where are you going, sir?'

'I'm going to the Airbase, to have a sniff around and see if anybody has any ideas.'

In St Ives Felicity was sitting in Annie Trethewey's cosy cottage tucked behind the harbour. She had accepted a cup of coffee and was now fighting a losing battle to avoid helping herself to one of Annie's legendary chocolate brownies.

'Oh, what the hell,' she said, grinning at Annie, 'it doesn't matter what I look like at my age.'

'There lies your trouble, my girl,' said Annie, firmly.

'What do you mean?' Felicity asked, behind a mouthful of brownie.

'You need to have a bit more faith in yourself. You may not be young but you're still pretty as a picture and despite my best efforts there's not a spare ounce on you. You've got years of life ahead of you, you've raised your children and it's time you started thinking about yourself and what you want, and above all having some fun.'

'You mean I shouldn't be helping Mel with

Minty?' Felicity asked.

While Annie had been making the coffee, Felicity had given her a blow-by-blow account of the problem with Mel and babysitting.

Annie shook her wise old head. 'No, I'm not saying that at all, my lover. You look after Minty twenty-four hours a day, seven days a week if it's what you want to do. God love her, she's a sweet little thing, but you're right to consider whether you want the commitment.'

Felicity nodded. 'I just feel so selfish about having any doubts and clearly that's what Mel thinks, too. Most women in my circumstances would give anything in the world to have a beautiful little granddaughter on their doorstep.' She hesitated. 'And I do love it, the thought of being a part of her growing up. But quite apart from the commitment issue, I'm not sure I should be making Mel's return to work too easy.'

Annie propped her head on one side. 'How do you mean?'

'Well, you and I, Annie, when we had our babies, it would never have occurred to either of us to work while our children were very small.'

Annie gave a bark of laughter. 'What, not work? I never worked so hard in my life as when my boys were small.'

'You know what I mean,' said Felicity, 'out to work, a job outside the home and marriage.'

Annie considered the question. 'They're missing out so much, these young people, not raising their own children,' she conceded. She gave Felicity a shrewd look. 'But I wouldn't worry about Mel's decision, it's just that, hers. Knowing your Mel as I do, if she has decided she's going to go back to work then that is what she is going to do and if you won't look after Minty, she'll find someone who will. There's no stopping that young lady when she's got a plan she intends to carry out.'

'That's very true,' Felicity conceded. The thought depressed her and she felt suddenly anxious to change the subject. 'Annie, tell me all the gossip about the fire in Back Road West.'

'Arson wasn't it, so I understand?' said Annie. 'Your inspector has been to have a look, I'm told, so it must be serious.'

'He did pop in to see me,' Felicity admitted. 'It's a nasty business. The whole street could have gone up as I understand it. Do you know the couple who lost their cottage?'

'I don't,' said Annie, 'but my daughter-in-law, Morwenna, Tim's girl, she does the changeover for them. They let it for part of the year but they always come down for Christmas and the New Year and other times, too. Their son uses it, as well. It's a nice cottage, or at least it was, Morwenna is well put out that her Saturday job has gone.'

'So they're not the sort of people who anybody would have a grudge against?' Felicity asked.

'Aah,' said Annie, 'so your inspector does reckon it's arson, then?'

'I don't think he's sure,' Felicity said, immediately defensive, conscious that she should not be discussing her conversation with Keith.

'So you're not going to tell me what Chief Inspector Penrose thinks,' said Annie, who missed nothing. 'Well, despite that, I will tell you what I know which is precious little. Their names are Brian and Elspeth Turner and they have one son, Gary, who is a helicopter pilot over at Culdrose. They come down here to stay when he has a bit of leave. That's probably the reason they don't let the cottage through an agent, they have a website apparently, gives them more flexibility as to when they choose to stay down here themselves. Morwenna deals direct with them, they pay her regular, trust her to replace things that get broken and always give her a box of goodies at Christmas for the family. Good as gold they are, I can't see no one having anything against them.'

'That's strange,' said Felicity, 'because if it is arson, what possible reason could anyone have to set fire to their cottage, unless of course it's not about them but what they stand for?'

'Might be because they're incomers,' said Annie. 'Some people don't like incomers.'

'That's what Keith thought initially, but he doesn't think so now.'

'Well, whatever the reason it's terrible for them,' said Annie.

'I always think it must be awful to lose all the little bits and pieces of life, not so much the valuable things,' said Felicity.

'Yes,' Annie agreed.

'Like those awful bits of pottery that your children made at primary school.'

'It's funny the things you treasure,' said Annie, smiling. 'I have a crucifix, I'm not particularly religious, as you know, but my mother gave it to me when I was very small to hang on the wall in the bedroom I shared with my sister. I've had it with me ever since, couldn't bear to lose it. It's only a cheap old thing made of tin but it means everything to me.'

'Charlie's bookmarks,' Felicity said. 'That's my equivalent.'

'How come?' Annie asked.

'When Mel was little she made a lot of bookmarks – cross-stitch on canvas, you know the sort of thing. Her idea was to set up a bookmark business and sell them. Being Mel, who does everything flat out, she made masses of the things and she sold quite a few but she ended up with six she couldn't sell so Charlie bought them. In fact he found them invaluable. Whenever he was working on a case, he'd have his law notes spread out everywhere with Mel's bookmarks marking his reference points instead of scruffy bits of paper. When he died I gave his law notes to the library of his old college but the bookmarks are in my bedside drawer. I use one of them, with whatever book I'm reading; they're very comforting.'

'You need a new man in your life, my girl,' said

Annie, 'then you wouldn't have time for bookmarks.'

Felicity stood up to go, laughing. 'Don't start that again, Annie.'

'I'm starting nothing,' said Annie, 'just saying what's true.' They climbed the stairs together from Annie's basement kitchen to the front door. 'You remember what I said,' Annie insisted firmly as they embraced by the front door. 'Put yourself first. Don't let that Mel boss you about. Do what feels right.'

'What would I do without you, Annie?' Felicity said, smiling.

'I really don't know, my bird,' Annie answered, with engaging honesty.

Chief Inspector Penrose had spent a frustrating morning at Culdrose Airbase. It was not that they had been uncooperative – far from it, they had fallen over backwards to be helpful but he had come away empty-handed. No one seemed to have a grudge against the Base, there had been no hate mail as long as anyone could remember. It was generally recognised that they did a vital job – 'saving people from themselves' was how it had been described to Keith.

'You wouldn't believe what people get up to, the risks they take, the danger in which they place themselves and their children,' the Commanding Officer had told him.

So the Base provided a vital service and made an enormous difference to the economy of the area, hardly grounds for resentment.

Keith had studied the records of rescue-based incidents around St Ives going back over several years. Virtually all of the rescues were successful. There was one which caught Keith's eye – two children in a rubber dinghy in the Hayle estuary, notorious for its currents. The officer helping him had shaken his head sadly. 'What the parents thought they were doing, God knows. The children were small,' he consulted the notes, 'six and four. The current took them, swept them out into the bay and the parents didn't seem to notice, thought they were having fun. By the time we were alerted, the dinghy had capsized. We found them very quickly, it was a beautiful clear sunny day. We winched them both aboard, the little girl we managed to resuscitate but the little boy had been dead for some time.'

'Is it possible the parents could have blamed you in some way, shifted the blame onto you because they couldn't cope with the responsibility for their son's death?' Keith asked, knowing he was clutching at straws.

The officer shook his head. 'I don't think so. At the inquest they were told in no uncertain terms that another five minutes and they'd have lost both children. I remember them expressing their gratitude to the crew in the press at the time. They knew there was nothing more we could have done.'

Keith thought about the two children as he swung his car onto the Falmouth road towards Truro. He imagined the four-year-old boy happily paddling about on a clear summer's day, with death just around the corner. The image made him think of his own son, Billy – no, – Will he must remember to call him that now. He had never been an easy child, given to tantrums and constant arguments with his sister. His wife, Barbara, always said he was too soft on the boy but Keith hated confrontation in the home, he had enough of it at work. Maybe he should have been harder on him; certainly it would appear that he and Barbara had failed him in some way. Will was home, yes, but wouldn't discuss anything, tell them his plans or explain to them what had happened. He'd left the Army was all that he would say but his contract still had another two years to run; Keith just couldn't make it out. Then there was his friend, Nick, who also seemed to have been discharged. Nick was living in Redruth now and instinctively Keith didn't like him, didn't trust him, although he had never met him. When Nick came to pick Will up for a session at the pub he always stayed in the car; odd. And that was another thing, Will coming in at all hours drunk, noisy, upsetting his mother. He was a man now, not a teenager, they should have been through all that. Keith was just relieved that Will's sister, Carly, was no longer living at home. She'd hardly seen her brother since his return though she was coming for lunch this Sunday. Sparks would fly, Keith was sure of that and equally sure that he would want to be anywhere else but at home.

4

Martin Tregonning was Felicity's son-in-law. He had also been her friend since before he had met Mel. He was fourteen years older than Mel putting him as close in age to mother as to daughter. He was good-looking in a rugged, slightly bohemian, sort of way; he was also friendly and caring and Felicity knew she was very lucky to have him as part of the family and even luckier that Mel had married someone who could handle her headstrong ways. The bond between Martin and Felicity was much deeper than it might otherwise have been because they had something in common. Within a few months of Martin losing his first wife in a car crash Felicity's husband, Charlie, had died in a hit-and-run. In both cases the death of their partner had come out of the blue. There was no preparation for it; shock was added to the devastation of their loss and it was in those early months of pain that they had first met. They never talked of it now. Martin, in any case, had moved on with a new wife and a baby, but it remained an unspoken link between them.

Felicity picked her way across the path separating the raised beds. 'Martin,' she called. 'Are you there?'

'Over here,' he called from the first row of polytunnels.

'Come on now, Archie, and behave yourself,' Felicity instructed the extraordinary-looking mongrel she had on the end of a tatty old lead. Large brown eyes regarded her kindly, with just a hint of compassion.

'Fizzy, hello, how are you?' said Martin, emerging from the polytunnel. He held a trowel in one hand and seemed to be largely covered in compost. 'How lovely to see you.' He stopped in his tracks, 'Good Lord, who on earth is this?'

'This is Archie,' said Felicity. 'I'm babysitting him for a few days while his parents are away.'

'Parents?' Martin said.

'Well, owners then,' Felicity corrected. 'Though I have to say Henry and Ursula treat him more like a child than a dog, and with good reason. He is extremely intelligent, aren't you Archie?'

Archie acknowledged the compliment with a dignified wag of the tail, which itself was an extraordinary sight, set pointing straight upwards like a poodle but managing to be long and feathery like a retriever.

'Well, he would need to be looking like that,' Martin said, with a not unkind smile.

'Please Martin, not in front of Archie, he's very sensitive.'

Martin laughed. 'Now I would embrace you but you'd probably rather I didn't, so would you and Archie like a cup of tea and a biscuit, instead?'

Felicity regarded Martin with affection. 'Certainly I'm happy to forego the hug but we'd love to accept your hospitality.'

'Follow me to my shed then,' said Martin. While he fussed over the kettle and Archie appreciatively crunched on a digestive biscuit, Felicity asked about the Nursery. Martin was into his second season of running his own business, a dodgy time.

'Actually,' he said, 'it's going really well. I think specializing helps, it brings people from all over the Duchy and beyond. I'm setting up an online mail order business too, not for big plants just plugs, but I think it should go well.'

'So you're sticking to exotic sub-tropical plants?' Felicity asked.

'More or less, yes,' Martin said, 'I'm trying to sell things that no one else is offering on a regular basis but I also have to bear in mind that Cornwall enjoys a better climate for sub-tropical plants than anywhere else in the country, except of course Scilly, so my plants have to be hardy, too. It means unfortunately I have to spend hours and hours doing what I love best.'

'Which is?' Felicity said with a smile.

'Pouring over gardening catalogues, it drives Mel mad.'

'I can imagine,' said Felicity.

'Which, of course,' said Martin shrewdly,

handing Felicity a cracked, none-too-clean mug, 'is why you're here, it's about Mel going back to work, I assume.'

Felicity nodded. 'Before I agree to anything,' she said, 'I thought I should see how you feel about it. I don't want that to sound as if I'm going behind Mel's back, it's just that she's so adamant that this is what she's going to do and it's a big step with so young a baby. I'm on my way to see her now, actually, and I just thought I should talk it through with you first. I hope you don't think I'm being disloyal.'

Martin shook his head. 'No, just caring and in answer to your question, I am totally supportive of Mel's desire to go back to work. I think to stop her would make her very frustrated and unsettled.'

'It's not good for her to always have her own way,' Felicity suggested.

Martin smiled, ruefully. 'Can you ever remember a time when she didn't get her own way?'

Felicity laughed. 'No, not really, but is it right for Minty?'

'I think the question you have to ask yourself,' said Martin, 'is whether it is right for you. Minty will be fine.'

'That's what Annie said,' Felicity admitted.

'And Annie is a wise old bird if ever there was one,' said Martin.

'I think I could be happy with two days a week,' Felicity said, 'I just think three's rather a big commitment.'

'My thoughts exactly,' said Martin, 'and my boy can cover the Nursery for one day a week, so I can look after Minty. In fact we don't even have to make it two days for you and one for me every week. If you need time off I'll cover for you and if I have a crisis in the Nursery maybe you'd occasionally cover for me.'

'Sounds perfect,' said Felicity. 'Sounds like we're going to let the wretched child get her own way then.'

Martin smiled. 'It rather looks like it. Another biscuit Archie?' Archie accepted the hospitality with considerable enthusiasm.

The cottage that Martin and Mel shared was not a thing of beauty, a little two-up, two-down pebbledash affair with a tiny garden surrounded by a dilapidated picket fence, but it was the view which saved it. Perched on the very edge of the Saltings, from every window you could see views out to sea and towards St Ives Bay. Mel answered the door looking fraught and upset; in the background Minty could be heard screaming.

'Who's that?' said Mel, glaring at Archie.

'Archie,' Felicity replied. 'I'm babysitting him for a few days.'

Mel turned her back and flounced into the cottage. 'Happy to babysit a weird-looking dog but not your own granddaughter.'

'Don't be silly, Mel,' said Felicity, as she and Archie followed her daughter into the cottage.

'I'm not being silly,' Mel began, 'I'm …' and

promptly burst into tears. Mel didn't do tears. Felicity and Archie regarded her with concern and Felicity went to put her arms around her. Mel shook off her mother's embrace. 'I'm OK.' Felicity looked beyond her daughter and into the kitchen where Minty was lying in her carrycot screaming her head off.

'What's wrong with Minty?' she asked.

'It's all my fault,' said Mel, tearfully. 'My milk's dried up; I've just got nothing there for her. She's hungry, poor thing.' Mel went to the baby and picked her up, rubbing her back and gently rocking her. The crying eased to a few little heartbreaking sobs. Archie had followed Felicity into the kitchen and stood, staring up at the baby, his face creased with worry.

'Look Minty,' said Felicity. 'A dog.' She sat at the kitchen table and taking one of Minty's hands stroked Archie's head, which he'd laid carefully on Felicity's knee so that the baby could reach it.

'See, even that bloody dog would make a better mother than me,' Mel wailed. 'I don't know what to do, Mum.'

'Don't be so hard on yourself, Mel, not everyone can manage breastfeeding long-term. You've given Minty several weeks of goodness but as you're going back to work, it would be a lot easier for everyone if we put her on the bottle.'

'As I'm going back to work?' Mel asked. 'You mean you're prepared to …'

'I've talked to Martin,' said Felicity, 'and we've agreed to cover three days a week between us.'

'Oh, Mum, thank you.' The words were warm and genuine. Mel knelt down by Minty, still sitting on Felicity's lap and stared at the baby. 'I am right, aren't I, she's hungry?'

'Looks like it,' said Felicity. 'Come on, let's put her in the pram and you and I and Archie will walk into town and buy some formula milk.'

A couple of hours later, peace was restored. Minty, with a full tummy, was blissfully asleep in her cot, Felicity had made a stew for supper and Mel having caught up on an hour's sleep, joined her for a cup of tea looking hugely refreshed.

'You're not a bad old trout sometimes, are you?' said Mel, affectionately.

Felicity smiled at her. 'I do my best.'

'You still don't approve of me going back to work, do you, even though you're prepared to help?'

'It's not a question of approving or disapproving. You're doing what you feel is right for you. Your husband supports you and that's all there is to be said.'

'They've sent me a brief already,' said Mel. 'It's an interesting case. My client is the father of three children, or at least two for sure.'

'How does that work?' Felicity asked, frowning.

'He and his wife split up at the time of the birth of the third child, which she claims is not his though she won't name the father. She won't let him near any of the children, maintaining that he is a danger to them, but there's no evidence of that. He hasn't seen any of the children for nineteen months, he misses them terribly. He's not trying to gain custody, just reasonable access and he doesn't mind whether the baby is his or not, he's a sibling to his own children and that's all that matters to him.'

'He sounds a nice chap. So, when are you meeting him?' Felicity asked.

Mel had the grace to look shamefaced. 'Well, I was rather hoping it could be tomorrow.'

It was ten days later that Felicity was retelling the story of Mel's return to work to Keith Penrose over lunch at Bustopher's Wine Bar in Truro.

'Some people just thrive on work and Mel's one of them,' said Felicity. 'She's sort of lit up by it. Without it, she seems lost. I'm not saying she doesn't love Minty and I'm not saying she's not going to make a good mother, but motherhood isn't her raison d'etre, it is just part of what she is. I rather envy her.'

'Why's that?' Keith asked.

Felicity smiled a little wistfully. 'I've rather lived my life through other people and I slightly despise myself for it.'

'Not *through* other people,' Keith corrected, '*for* other people, surely.'

Felicity shook her head. 'My career naturally took second place to Charlie's. Charlie was already a qualified lawyer when we married and apart from any other consideration, he was earning proper money and I was just a struggling artist. Then, when the children came along both he and I felt it important to have a mother around, so I simply fitted my life around theirs. Teaching art seemed to be the best way to go so that I was free when they were free. Only now I'm feeling a bit of a wimp seeing Mel having it all, as it were, I should have been more assertive.'

'I think it's a generation thing,' said Keith. 'My wife, Barbara, was the same. She has a big job now, running the planning department, but when the children were growing up, she was a full-time mum. People were then – now it's not rated as a job. I don't know who's right, them or us, I just know it's different and whatever we do and whoever we are, if we're parents, we always feel we could have done a better job.'

Felicity smiled at him. 'You're a wise old thing aren't you, Chief Inspector?'

'Less of the old, but it is a point and something you mustn't beat yourself up about. Take my boy, Will. He seems to have turned into a thoroughly nasty piece of work, rude to his mother and me, coming home drunk most nights, showing no inclination to get a job or do anything even vaguely responsible and, of course, so far as I'm concerned, it's all my fault. I was so busy policing during his childhood he virtually grew up without a father – at least that's what Barbara says, and I expect she's right, she usually is. We had an awful Sunday lunch last weekend.'

'Why, what happened?' Felicity asked.

'Carly was home.'

'Is she alright?' Felicity asked, interrupting. Keith's daughter had bravely fought off cancer the year before.

'Fine, still in remission, fingers crossed. Anyway, she was home. She and Will had a terrible row. She told him he was a useless layabout and was treating us like dirt and he told her to, well I won't tell you what he told her to do. It was awful.'

'So what did you do?' Felicity asked.

'You don't want to know.'

'I do,' she persisted.

'I took the dog for a walk.'

Felicity laughed out loud. 'Do you know, Chief Inspector, I had never had you down as a coward.'

'Well there you go, Mrs Paradise, you can't always be right.' They smiled fondly at one another.

'Families,' said Felicity, 'they're so complicated, aren't they?'

'And never what they seem,' said Keith. 'If I've learned anything from my years in the force, it's that the most difficult thing to form an accurate opinion about is how someone else's family works – and certainly almost impossible to sit in judgement.'

'And that's what Mel's chosen to do with her career, isn't it?' said Felicity. 'She is going to spend her entire working life trying to sort out the tangled web families make for themselves. Sort it out, make it better, paper over the cracks, heal the wounds.'

'Rather her than me,' said Keith, at which point his mobile phone rang. 'Excuse me,' he said, 'sorry.'

He answered the phone, smiling, but as he listened the smile left his face along with the colour. Felicity watched the transformation with horror. 'Where?' Keith said. 'When? I'll be right there.' He turned off his phone and rose to his feet. 'I'm sorry,' he stumbled over the words, 'I'm going to have to go, there's been another arson attack.'

'Oh, no,' said Felicity.

'The bill,' Keith began, 'I'll just go and ...'

'Leave it,' said Felicity. 'It's my turn anyway. You go, where is the fire?'

'Just outside St Ives again, Halsetown, only this one is different, people have died,' he said, his voice choked with emotion, 'children.'

Chief Inspector Keith Penrose's horror of children suffering was the stuff of legend across Devon and Cornwall's Constabulary, so when he appeared from the burnt-out doorway of the still smouldering cottage, his face ashen, his walk unsteady, no one was surprised. Jack, suddenly protective, came forward to meet him.

'I told you not to go in there, sir,' he said quietly.

'Don't be an idiot,' said Keith, sharply, 'I had to, you know I did.' Slowly he passed a trembling hand through his hair. 'Do we know if the fire was started like the others?'

'Too early to tell,' said Jack. 'As you can see the forensic boys are on it already but the trouble is,' he hesitated, 'this one's so badly burnt I think it's going to be difficult to establish how the fire was started. With the others the firelighters were quite easy to trace; in fact in two of the cottages, as you remember, there were traces on the letterbox as they were pushed through.' His voice sounded strained. 'This time not only is there no evidence of a letterbox, but there's no sign of a front door either.'

'We've got to get the bastard who's doing this. I blame myself. I was too complacent, just because nobody's been hurt before now ... those children. When was the fire started?

'About five o'clock this morning, they reckon.'

'So why did it take you so long to contact me?'

'Well, as you can see, the cottage is quite isolated so it took a while for anyone to spot it at that hour. Then the fire brigade arrived, they had a mammoth task on their hands to put it out and assumed that it was another empty cottage. That is until the neighbours started appearing enquiring about the children.'

'I want every available man on this, Jack,' Keith said. 'Set up an incident room, and I want everyone back at the station by three o'clock this afternoon. So the victims are a mother and her three children but what about the father? Where is he? Why wasn't he here?'

'We're on to it, sir. Hopefully there will be something to report by the time we get back to the station.'

Felicity sat in her cottage watching the local six o'clock news on Spotlight. No names had been released as to the identity of the victims as yet, but they were described as an adult woman and three children, one only a baby, burnt to death in their cottage. She could only imagine how Keith felt about the scene he must have had to witness. She leaned forward to turn off the television and at the same time the telephone rang. She picked it up. It was Mel.

'Mum, did you see the news?' She sounded distraught.

'Yes I did, you mean the fire at Halsetown?'

'Yes, yes,' said Mel. 'The family who died, they're the family of my client, David Belcher. The police have just arrested him, they think he was responsible for the fire. You don't know him Mum, he's just such a gentle soul, he couldn't possibly have done a thing like that. Please get hold of your inspector and tell him he's wrong.'

'Mel, I can't possibly,' Felicity said. 'Our relationship doesn't work like that.'

'Yes it does, you're always putting him straight when he gets a case wrong.'

'No, I'm not,' Felicity said, 'though I must admit, I'm surprised he has arrested your client – what did you say his name was?'

'David Belcher.'

'There have been a string of arson attacks as you know. This is the fifth cottage to be burnt down. It sounds unlikely that your client would have been responsible for all the fires. If the thinking is he killed his family out of some sort of desperate revenge, the police must believe the fire is unconnected to the others.'

'Mum, he's not responsible for any of the fires. He's not a nutter, he's just a nice bloke who wanted to see his kids – your inspector has got the wrong man.'

'They may have just asked him in for questioning,' Felicity said. 'He is the next-of-kin.'

'No, he's definitely been arrested. Our senior partner, Arthur O'Sullivan who deals in criminal law, is representing him. Please do something, Mum, please.'

5

Chief Inspector Keith Penrose silently handed over his neatly-pressed, pristine white handkerchief to the broken man sitting opposite him.

'I'll organise you some more coffee, Mr Belcher.' He motioned to Jack and the man's solicitor to follow him out of the room. 'Stay with him Constable, he shouldn't be left alone even for a moment.' The young policeman looked uneasy in the face of such grief. At the door Keith glanced over his shoulder at the man now sobbing into his handkerchief. Then, with a sigh, he strode out of the room and headed down the corridor. 'Arthur, Jack, come to my office,' he commanded. In his office Keith moved some piles of paper around so both men could sit down.

Keith and Arthur O'Sullivan of Sullivan and Stoat were old sparring partners. Arthur, a criminal defence lawyer, had tangled with Keith on many occasions in the past.

'Keith, this is harassment,' he began. 'My client

is in no fit state to be cross-examined and in any event what possible grounds do you have for holding him?'

Keith sat down heavily at his desk. 'Absolutely none, Arthur and no, it's not harassment, because I'm releasing him.'

'What!' said Jack jumping up. 'Sir, he was in the area, he was seen drinking heavily at the Halsetown Inn just hours before the fire. He has a clear motive, he couldn't see his children and had just learnt his wife had taken up with a new man – if he couldn't have them, no one else could either. How can you let him go?'

'Because he didn't do it, Jack,' said Keith.

'Good Lord,' said Arthur, 'the man is talking sense for once.'

Keith ignored him. 'I appreciate there's a great deal of circumstantial evidence, Jack, but David Belcher is a decent bloke who clearly adored his children. He wouldn't have hurt a hair on their head let alone burnt them to a crisp.' Keith swallowed; the image of what he had seen at the Halsetown cottage was still horrifyingly fresh in his mind. 'Tell him he's free to go and say Arthur will be with him in a moment to take him home.' Keith looked at Arthur. 'I'll need his passport and I don't want him leaving the Duchy.'

Arthur nodded. 'You're doing the right thing, Keith.'

'I know,' said Keith. Jack left the room, shutting

the door none-too-quietly and the two men sat in silence for a moment or two. 'I shouldn't have arrested him,' Keith said, 'it was an overreaction, the sight of those children …'

'I appreciate my client is the obvious candidate, Keith; just not the right one,' said Arthur, smugly.

'It's just hard to imagine who would do such a thing. The family car was outside, whoever set fire to the house must have known there were people inside it, children too – there was a swing and a slide in the garden.' Keith shook his head as if trying to shake away the images which crowded into his mind.

'I presume you've considered the new man in Sarah Belcher's life,' Arthur asked.

Keith nodded. 'His name is Harry Jones, he's a salesman in vending machines. He met Sarah at the Halsetown Inn, apparently. Since she and David split up, she had been working there part time in the evenings to make a bit of extra money – her mother did the babysitting. Jones stayed on for a drink one night having installed a new machine, that's how they met. He covers a wide area, the whole of the West Country. On the night of the fire he had just installed a vending machine in a pub on the outskirts of Bath and was chatting up the barmaid there too. Poor Sarah, at least she never had to know what sort of man Jones truly was – at least I hope she didn't.'

'So if Jones didn't set fire to that cottage, is there no one else who could have had some sort of grudge?'

Keith shrugged. 'You tell me, Arthur. I gather

from my sergeant that David's mother is still alive – have you met her? Is she the sort of person who would kill her grandchildren, if such a person exists?'

'No,' said Arthur, 'she's very like David, a gentle sort of woman, riddled with arthritis too. I wouldn't have thought there was a hope in hell of her even getting to the cottage without help.'

'So,' said Keith, getting to his feet, 'we know we're looking for a monster but first of all, I have to find a motive.'

Arthur rose too and held out his hand. 'No doubt you'll get your man, Keith.'

Keith smiled, grimly. 'And then I'll get him into court, only for you to have him acquitted or given some greatly reduced sentence for mitigating circumstances or some such rubbish.' He met Arthur O'Sullivan's eye, unable to disguise his bitterness. 'You'll look after your client, will you? In my view he's a danger to himself at the moment.'

'I'm going to choose to ignore what you just said, Keith,' Arthur replied, pompously, 'and yes, I am aware of my client's state of mind. I'll take him back to his mother's house and stay with him until his GP can come around and give him something.'

'What about the press?' said Keith. 'They're going to be hounding him, aren't they?'

'I haven't said anything to them, yet,' said Arthur, 'have you?'

Keith shook his head.

'Then let's just play down the arrest, shall we?'

said Arthur, smoothly, 'for both our sakes. It will save you the humiliation of having to admit to a wrongful arrest and spare my client's feelings. It was inevitable you asked him in for questioning; it was his family who died, after all. Let's try and leave it at that.'

Keith did not trust himself to respond.

Jack Curnow was sulking and by lunchtime Keith's patience was at an end. 'We have enough problems, Jack, without you behaving like some spoilt brat.'

'I'm sorry, sir,' said Jack. They were in the corridor by the coffee machine. 'I just think ...' Jack began.

'Well don't,' said Keith.

'It's just that David Belcher had the motive and he was in the area. We also know he had a skinful at the pub less than a quarter of a mile from the cottage. I am prepared to admit he probably didn't know what he was doing – he was just angry and very drunk.'

'He didn't do it, Jack.'

'I'm not even saying he's not sorry for what he's done, devastated even,' Jack began, 'you saw the state he was in.'

'Jack, would you drop it please. Instead of wasting time with David Belcher, you should be thinking about the real villain.'

'I just hope you're right.'

'I am right,' said Keith. 'I've had the Super on to me twice this morning, wanting to know what progress we're making. "Five fires, Keith, and not a single lead" was his running theme. Can't you imagine what a relief it would have been to find Belcher was our man?' Keith picked up his coffee cup and started back towards his office.

'Oh, sir, there was a message for you from Culdrose.'

'Yes,' said Keith, wearily.

'You showed some interest in an incident in the Hayle Estuary, a little boy died apparently.'

'I haven't got time for this now, Jack.'

'OK,' said Jack. 'The message was that the Base thought you might like to know the coastguard on the scene was Martin Tregonning, in case you wanted to talk to him. Isn't he …'

'Yes,' said Keith, wearily, 'he's Mrs Paradise's son-in-law.'

By five-thirty the following afternoon Keith Penrose was in despair. Every available man had been employed to do house-to-house enquiries, stop and question drivers on the Halsetown road – nobody had seen anything or knew anything.

'The trouble is,' said Doctor Horace Greenaway, the head of forensics, during Keith's third call to him of the day, 'arson is always a tricky business, the fire so often destroys the evidence – obvious, I know, but always makes for an unsatisfactory report. The woman, God bless her, burnt to death trying to put out the flames. The children, mercifully, died of asphyxiation before the flames reached them – some comfort there, at least. But, as to where the fire started – the ground floor of the cottage was open plan – kitchen, sitting room, dining room, one big room. Whether an arsonist posted something in the letterbox like on the other occasions I don't think we'll ever know. That's my honest view, Keith, I'm sorry.'

'Horace, surely to God you can give me something,' Keith said.

'I wish I could old boy. Believe me, we're leaving no stone unturned, the team are very upset by all this.'

'Aren't we all,' said Keith.

The offices were empty, Jack had gone home. Keith lifted the telephone and dialled Felicity Paradise's number.

'I've been thinking about you all day,' she said.

'Thinking what an idiot I am for not having found who's responsible?' he suggested.

'No, not that. I know how much the deaths of those children will have upset you.'

His tone softened. 'You're right about that, thanks. Actually, I was ringing to ask for Martin Tregonning's telephone number.'

'Good Lord,' said Felicity, 'you don't think he's involved in any of this, do you?'

'No, of course not,' said Keith. 'I just want to talk to him about an incident back in 2002 – a little boy drowned in the Hayle Estuary. Martin was the coastguard involved in the incident. I just wanted to talk to him about it, see what he can remember.'

'Is the little boy drowning related to the fire?' Felicity asked. 'Don't answer that if you don't want to, but you know I'm insatiably curious.'

'I had noticed, Mrs Paradise,' said Keith, smiling properly for the first time that day. 'To assuage your curiosity, I can tell you there is a common denominator with the first four fires, but not this latest one.'

'Really,' said Felicity, 'well, that's progress.'

'Not really, all the owners of the cottages, with the exception of the poor Belchers, had a connection to Culdrose Air Base. I've been to the Base, of course, and we have been looking for an incident involving Culdrose which might have caused a feeling of vengeance. The only rescue I could turn up in the St Ives area was this incident with the little boy. Culdrose don't reckon there was any problem. The parents were well aware of their own stupidity in letting the child and his sister go out in a rubber dinghy. They were grateful to Culdrose for saving the sister. Nonetheless, that is the Base's take on it. I wouldn't mind finding out what Martin feels about it.'

Felicity gave him Martin's telephone number. 'If you go to see him tomorrow, Thursday or Friday you'll find me there; I'm babysitting Minty, so you could come in for a coffee afterwards.'

'I'm not sure I'll have the time to see him,' said

Keith. 'I'll probably just telephone him, but thanks anyway.'

'Good luck with your enquiries, Chief Inspector,' said Felicity.

'Thanks,' said Keith, 'I have a feeling I'm going to need it.'

Felicity's much loved cat, Orlando, had been dead now for nearly a year. For months she had mourned him and missed the presence of an animal in her home, but felt quite unable to replace him in any way. A cat had been an excellent companion in North Oxford but here, in St Ives, she had already decided that she would share her life with a dog this time, though it would have to be a small dog. She had been reading *The Cornishman* when Keith telephoned and afterwards she returned to it, circling the advertisement she had seen for rough-haired Jack Russell puppies. There was a Penzance telephone number. She rang the number and soon established that there were still plenty of puppies available, both dogs and bitches, and that the farm where they had been born was in Halsetown.

The farmer's wife, Mary Jennings, gave her directions from the Halsetown Inn. 'You'll know you're on the right track because you'll pass the burnt-out cottage. You heard about our tragedy?'

'Oh, yes,' said Felicity.

'Well, just keep on going past the cottage and you'll come to our farm, you can't miss it.' They arranged that Felicity should visit the following morning at ten o'clock.

As she started down the farm track, the cottage's silhouette appeared on the horizon. It stood alone on high ground, a ghastly skeleton. As she drew nearer to it, Felicity saw there was still plenty of activity. The area was cordoned off with police tape and there were men in white suits sifting through the rubble. She tried to shut out of her mind the image of the desperate woman trying to save her children and drove on towards the farm.

Mary Jennings was delightful, a children's storybook idea of a farmer's wife; overweight and of middle years she nonetheless had an obvious energy and health about her, with traditional apple cheeks, warm twinkling brown eyes and a floral pinny protecting her ample form.

The puppies were snuggled with their mother in an old box in front of the Aga. Felicity played with them while Mary made coffee.

'It seems awful to take one away from its mother,' Felicity said.

'They're not ready yet, my dear, not for another couple of weeks. By then their mother will be longing to be rid of them, believe me. Do you want a dog or a bitch?'

'A dog, I think,' said Felicity. 'I fancy this little chap.'

'He's the runt of the litter,' said Mary, 'I was going to knock twenty pounds off for him.'

'He's healthy though, isn't he?'

'Oh yes, they're pedigree dogs; they're registered with the Kennel Club but I'm not sure he'll be much good for showing or breeding.'

'I just want him as a friend,' said Felicity, standing up the puppy in her arms. He was licking her face.

'Then I reckon he'll do the job,' said Mary, smiling. 'Has he got a name?'

'Not yet,' said Felicity, 'I'm working on it.' Felicity returned the puppy to its mother and the two women sat at the kitchen table while Felicity wrote out a cheque. 'Awful, that fire,' she said.

'Yes,' said Mary, 'I didn't know them well, kept themselves to themselves, but a nice woman by all accounts and lovely little kids – terrible. The cottage used to belong to us, you know. We sold it to the Belchers a few years back when Sarah was expecting the first one, Bethany. Lovely young couple they were then, so happy with their first baby on the way … and to think how it ended.'

'Have you any ideas who could have started the fire?' Felicity asked.

'As I told the police, not a clue,' said Mary, shaking her head. 'I know there's been some talk of the father being responsible, but he could never have done it, a nice man, devoted to those children. It was just sad they split up.'

'Why did they split up?' Felicity asked.

Mary shrugged. 'I don't know, just the way

people do. As Tom, my husband, said, whoever did that terrible thing chose the wrong cottage. We've got two others and they were both empty at the time. Pity it wasn't one of them, like what happened at Trencrom.'

'Who lives in your other cottages?' Felicity asked.

'One's a holiday let, the other we've let on a long tenancy to a travel writer. He's not here much, always off doing his travelling,' she smiled. 'He just comes down here to write up what he's seen.'

'What a wonderful job,' said Felicity, 'travelling the world and then writing about it in Cornwall. It sounds an ideal existence.'

'Yes, he loves Cornwall; he's not Cornish mind, but he's lived down here a long time. He used to be a helicopter pilot at Culdrose, but he's always loved writing and once he got his first book published he decided to write full time. We were happy to let him have the cottage on a low rent as …'

'He was at Culdrose?' Felicity interrupted.

Mary nodded curiously. 'Why?'

'Oh, no reason,' Felicity said, hurriedly. 'Look, I'd better not hold you up anymore. When will it be convenient to come and collect the puppy?'

'Week after next,' said Mary, 'same day, same time.'

'Perfect,' said Felicity.

'And give me a ring in the meantime when you decide on his name and we will start calling him by it.'

'Thanks.' Felicity bent over the box and picked up her puppy. 'We're going to have fun together, you and I,' she assured him.

'Keith, it's Felicity.'

'Hello,' said Keith, sounding absolutely exhausted.

'Look, this is probably nothing, but I've just been out to Halsetown.'

'Why?' Keith asked, abruptly.

'I went to see a puppy.'

'Thank goodness. I thought you might be one of those awful ghouls who go and look at the scenes of tragedy.'

'Oh, really,' said Felicity, 'you are the bloody limit sometimes Keith, surely you don't think I'm like that?'

'No, of course not, sorry, I'm just getting nowhere and taking it out on everybody.'

'Well, I have a little snippet for you,' said Felicity, 'though you've probably picked it up already.'

'I'm all ears,' said Keith, humbly, 'and grateful for anything.'

'The cottage that the Belchers owned, it used to belong to the farm further down the lane which belongs to some people called Tom and Mary Jennings.'

'I know,' said Keith.

'And they have two other cottages.'

'I know that too,' said Keith, with studied patience.

'Just bear with me,' said Felicity, irritated, 'don't be so dismissive.'

'Sorry, sorry,' said Keith.

'One is a holiday let and the other …'

'I know about the other,' said Keith. 'It's rented on a long lease to a travel writer called Philip Ferguson. I read his stuff, do you? He's very good. He's out East somewhere, Thailand I think, at the moment – certainly nowhere near the scene of the crime.'

'And do you know anything else about him?' said Felicity, trying to keep the note of triumph out of her voice.

'Nothing else to know, he's certainly not a suspect.'

'But he was a helicopter pilot at Culdrose Air Base.'

'What?' shouted Keith.

'Yes,' Felicity continued, 'he'd always wanted to be a writer apparently and as soon as his first book was published, he left the Navy to write full time.'

'None of the boys picked that up,' said Keith. 'It's absolutely ludicrous!'

'So I have my uses?' said Felicity.

'Yes, of course, you do – thanks. I just can't believe we missed it. It's my fault, knowing his work; he's so bloody good, I just presumed he'd always been a writer. I never thought to dig deeper.'

'So,' said Felicity, cutting through Keith's self-recrimination, 'what that means is the arsonist could have muddled up the cottages and set fire to the wrong one.'

'A good thought in theory,' said Keith, 'but until this last time, the arsonist has always gone for an empty cottage. Anyone with half a brain could see that the Belchers' cottage was occupied.'

'Even if they approached it from the back, coming across country?'

'I don't know,' said Keith, slowly, 'but I'll go and find out – in fact, I'll go and find out right now. Thanks again.'

'My pleasure,' said Felicity.

At three o'clock the following afternoon Keith presented himself at Tregonning's Nursery in Hayle. Martin, as usual, was covered in mud and compost and could not shake his hand.

'Chief Inspector,' he said, 'how nice to see you. Felicity said you'd be in touch. Can I get you a coffee or tea?'

Keith shook his head. 'I thought I'd go up to the house afterwards, if that's alright, and see Mrs Paradise. No doubt she'll make me one.'

'No doubt she will,' said Martin, 'you know she's babysitting Minty today?' Keith nodded. Martin wiped his hands on the back of his overalls. 'It's probably a wise decision anyway, the hygiene in my shed is somewhat suspect.'

Keith smiled. 'Definitely a good decision then. Martin, as I imagine Felicity will have told you, I'm here about those children in the rubber dinghy in the Hayle Estuary.'

'Jake and Daisy,' said Martin, his eyes suddenly clouding. 'Terrible.'

'You were involved, I understand.'

'Yes,' said Martin, 'in fact, I was the first on the scene. I had my float with me and was swimming out to the dinghy when the helicopter arrived, I helped them winch the children aboard.'

'The boy was already dead, I understand,' said Keith.

'Dead or dying,' said Martin. 'By the time I arrived, the dinghy had capsized and the little girl was trying to hold onto it and her brother, it was awful. I managed to turn the dinghy over and get her and the little boy back into it and the helicopter took them from there.'

'And the parents?'

'Neither of them could swim, would you believe?' said Martin. 'Yet they let their children out in a rubber dinghy, it was unreal.'

'Were they remorseful?' Keith asked.

'Yes, I'm sure they were,' said Martin. 'Obviously at the time of the incident they were extremely distraught,' he frowned, trying to remember. 'There was some sort of a conflict between them. Yes that's right, the father had gone back up to the car park and had been a long time coming back, why I can't remember. The mother had been left in charge and she was the dippy one who failed to see what was happening to the children. I didn't see the parents again. Once I got back on shore, the police had already taken them to Treliske Hospital.'

'Did they thank you or contact you again?'

Martin shook his head. 'No, I never heard from them again.'

'Bit odd that, isn't it?'

Martin considered the question. 'Well, not really, no. I was only part of the rescue.'

'Sounds to me like the little girl, Daisy you said her name was?' Martin again nodded his head.

'Sounds like Daisy wouldn't have made it without you. She wouldn't have been able to hold on much longer to her brother and the boat. She was only six, wasn't she?'

'Yes, that's probably true,' said Martin. 'I wish I'd made it in time to save her brother.'

'And you were at the inquest?'

'Yes, I had to give evidence.'

'And did they thank you afterwards?'

Martin shook his head. 'No, but they did thank the whole rescue service, which included me of course.'

'Do you think they are the sort of people who might have felt the rescue services should have done a better job?'

Martin considered the question in silence for a moment. 'I don't think so, no. They were not from round here, somewhere up North I think, on holiday of course. They clearly lived nowhere near the coast and had absolutely no idea of the danger they had put their children in. At the same time, I don't think their ignorance blinded them to the fact that they were very lucky to get their daughter back alive. Hard to tell, but I don't see them as people who thought we'd done an inadequate job. May I ask why, Chief Inspector?'

'We're looking for someone who might have a grudge against Culdrose Air Base.'

'Is this something to do with the arson attacks?' Martin asked. Keith nodded. 'Well I can't see them being the sort of couple that would go round burning houses down,' said Martin. 'To be perfectly honest, the husband was one of those smart Alecs who rather fancy themselves, the wife, poor thing, was not over-bright. I suspect neither of them would have the initiative.'

Keith smiled warmly. 'Well thanks for your help.'

'What a view!' A few minutes later Keith Penrose was standing in Martin Tregonning's kitchen, having been handed a mug of coffee by Felicity.

'Yes, it's a pretty ordinary little house, isn't it,' said Felicity, 'but the view is stunning. They picked it up quite cheap and hopefully in a year or two they'll be able to afford to extend it. It's a fantastic spot. Was Martin able to help?'

Keith shook his head. 'No, not really, he confirmed what I already knew – a terrible tragedy on a sunny summer's afternoon caused by parents ignoring all the signs and letting their children play in a dangerous current when, believe it or not, they couldn't even swim themselves.'

'Amazing. My father was in the Navy during the war,' said Felicity. 'He was always being blown up; he was involved in the Atlantic convoys. He said whatever the Germans threw at him, there was nothing so terrifying as the sea itself in a bad mood.'

'I agree with him,' said Keith. 'People just do not understand its power and on a sunny day it can look so …' he hesitated.

'Benevolent?' Felicity suggested.

'Exactly.'

'Are you getting anywhere with the case?' Felicity asked.

Keith shook his head. 'Not at all, except for your lead. You were right, incidentally.'

'About what?' Felicity asked.

'If you approached the Belchers' cottage from the far side, at night, it might not have been obvious that it was occupied.' He sighed and drank his coffee. 'The cottage is also very similar in shape and style to the cottage rented by Philip Ferguson. They're not quite a pair but they were probably built at the same time, by the same person. It would be very easy to mistake one for the other, even in daylight.'

'So the Belcher cottage could be the work of the arsonist?' Keith nodded. 'In which case he must be feeling terrible.'

'Certainly all the earlier fires suggested that the arsonist didn't want to hurt anyone … then to kill three little children.' Keith shook his head.

'Is there any forensic evidence to link it to the other fires?'

Keith shook his head. 'No, the cottage was too badly burnt. The forensic boys have been painstaking in trying to find some sort of evidence; they've all been very affected by the tragedy, but nothing so far.'

'And the press,' said Felicity, 'you've been worrying about that aspect?'

'At the moment the national press have picked up the story but they haven't linked it to the other arson attacks. I hate press speculation particularly over an emotive case like this one, but once they do make the link – and they will – they are going to have a field day. My superintendent is going nuts.'

'So you've come to ask me to have a look, have you?' Felicity said, quietly.

Keith studied her in silence for a moment. 'Yes,' he said, simply, 'but if you can't bear it, I completely understand. As you know, it's not really going to help the investigation in a tangible way because most of my colleagues think what you see is, well …' he hesitated. 'They're non-believers. Also anything you do see will never stand up as evidence. So please don't feel you've got to do this, because you haven't.'

Felicity turned her gaze from Keith to the window. A flock of geese was flying across the Saltings in perfect formation. As on so many occasions in the past, she wondered if it was a gift or a curse to sometimes see things no one else could. Her Oxford friends called it 'Fizzy's little moments', her husband and children had accepted it as just a part of her and never doubted her. Charlie had called it 'second sight' which she supposed was as good a description as any other. Before Charlie's death, her 'little moments' had been about the most mundane things. She would suddenly see some incident rerun before her but she had no control over it and she certainly couldn't call upon it when she needed it. 'Seeing' the moment of Charlie's death, not once but twice, seemed to have heightened her powers, if anything. Keith wanted her to visit the Belcher cottage. She had known from the moment she had heard the news that it was only a matter of time before he asked her. She had helped him before and she knew she would have to help him again. She turned from the window and met his eye.

'Yes, of course,' she said, 'of course I'll help you if I can, but you know there's no guarantee. I may see nothing.'

'Of course,' he said.

She smiled, trying to make light of the moment. 'You must really be desperate, Chief Inspector, to be asking for my help.'

'You're right,' he said, responding to her mood. 'I'm absolutely clutching at straws, very last resort.'

'Thanks a lot,' she said. 'So, when do you want to do this?'

'Do you want it to be dark?' he asked. 'It was dark at the time of the attack.'

'Dusk, certainly,' said Felicity, 'moving towards

dark. Dusk so we can get ourselves there, but once there, the darker the better.'

'Tonight?' Keith asked.

Felicity nodded.

'What time do you finish with Minty?'

'Oh, four o'clock this afternoon. Martin is coming in' she glanced at her watch, 'any minute now.'

'So about eight-thirty would be right for light.'

Felicity nodded. 'I hope I won't be a disappointment to you,' she said.

Keith stepped forward and gave her a quick, awkward hug. Drawing away he said 'You'll never be that. I just feel bad about putting you through this.'

Felicity looked at him, shrewdly. 'Visiting the scene is going to be as tough for you as it is for me, I suspect.'

Keith turned away, avoiding eye contact. 'Maybe,' he mumbled, as he hurried towards the front door. 'See you later,' he called.

Felicity stood by the front door chewing on her bottom lip. Would she really be able to see what had happened? The concept of seeing three children burn to death made her shudder. Minty began to whimper and gratefully Felicity shut the front door and hurried to absorb herself in tending to her granddaughter.

6

Keith had offered to pick her up from home and drive her to Halsetown but Felicity had decided it was better to travel alone. She was nervous, nervous of exposing herself to the horror that must have taken place inside the cottage and equally nervous that she might let Keith down, that she might see nothing at all or at least nothing that would be of any help. She bumped down the track to the cottage. Close to, the damage appeared even worse than it had done when she had seen it only as a skeleton on the hill; the roof was completely gone. She parked beside Keith's car. There was also a police car and as she looked towards the house she saw Keith talking to a uniformed policeman. Damn, she thought, I can't do this with an audience. On seeing her, Keith hurried down the path but Felicity's eyes were drawn away from him to the garden. There was a slide and a swing, a sandpit containing a few plastic spades and buckets, nearby a little wheelbarrow, a tiny trampoline: all the paraphernalia of childhood. Keith followed her gaze as he reached her.

'This garden,' Felicity gestured hopelessly, 'it's so untouched, it's as though any moment they'll be back out here to play.'

Keith put a hand on her shoulder. 'Look at me,' he insisted. She did so and met his kind, bright blue eyes. 'You don't have to do this. I've told PC Thompson,' he indicated towards the policeman at the door of the cottage, 'that you're a grieving relative who's come to have a look. If you want you can get back in your car and drive off, I'd completely understand.'

Felicity shook her head. 'No, I want to help, I really do, but we'll have to get rid of him.'

Keith nodded. 'If I ask him to sit in the car, will that do?'

'Fine,' said Felicity, 'as long as he stays there.' She squared her shoulders. 'Can we get around to the back of the cottage, I'm assuming that's the way you think the arsonist approached?'

Keith nodded. 'I'll just tell Thompson to wait in the car and then we'll walk up the lane, there's a stile there which will take us into the field and around to the back of the cottage. I've got a torch in my car too, I'll pick that up.'

Moments later they were walking down the lane. Keith helped her over the stile.

'As you can see,' he said, 'this field drops away down a very steep hill. Both the Belchers' cottage and the cottage belonging to Philip Ferguson are on top of the hill, to get to the bottom of this field, it's quite a slippery slide downhill and, more importantly, quite a climb back up. How far do you want to go?'

'I'd like to see where someone might have come into the field,' said Felicity, 'which presumably you've worked out.'

'Yes,' said Keith, 'there's a cart track which leads off the main lane, back near the road the way you came. It would be possible to drive a car down it. From that cart track there's a gate. Look, you can see it.' He pointed down the hill. 'It's a wide entrance as you can see, big enough for a tractor. It's the only way into the field. We've checked for car tyres, of course, but the problem is the farmer uses the track all the time, both for his tractor and his Land Rover. The rain over the last few days has churned it up so it's impossible to find anything. Nothing about this case is easy.'

They started down the hill towards the gate. Halfway down Felicity turned and looked up the hill. The valley where the cart track ran was almost in darkness but the sky was still light and the silhouette of the cottage, tragic and forlorn, stood out above them. She looked to the right and there, across the other side of the field, was a second cottage.

'That's Philip Ferguson's?' she asked.

Keith nodded. 'You were right, it could be easily done, to mistake one for the other, couldn't it?'

'Yes,' said Felicity, 'from the bottom of the hill

by the gate, I imagine you can barely see Philip's.' She was right; by the time they arrived at the muddy entrance to the field, Philip's cottage was no longer in view, but the Belchers' could still be seen clearly.

'In the dark,' said Felicity, 'it is easy to see how he would have simply homed in on the wrong cottage.'

'What do you want to do now?' said Keith.

'I want you to stay here,' said Felicity, 'and follow me up in a few minutes.' She smiled at him in the gathering gloom. 'And don't rush, Chief Inspector, you're a great deal fitter than me, it'll take me a while to trudge up this hill.'

'Poor old thing,' said Keith, lightly. 'I'll take into account your age and infirmity.'

'That's enough,' said Felicity, firmly.

'Do you want the torch?'

She shook her head. 'No, I can see enough. Give me a ten minute head start.'

It was a steep hill and the grass was slippery, and damp underfoot. She was glad of her walking boots. Her eyes had become accustomed to the gathering gloom so she had no problem in picking her way, but she was soon very out of breath. 'I need to walk more,' she thought, 'that puppy will be a good thing for me.' Halfway up the hill she paused, as much to get her breath as anything. Philip Ferguson's house was now in sight again but only, she realised, because there was some light in the sky. Flanked as it was by high hedges on both sides it would have blended into the darkness and been almost impossible to spot if it had been completely dark. By contrast the Belchers' cottage was still clearly a distinct shape on top of the hill. 'I must concentrate on the job in hand,' she thought as she started trudging again, 'not my wheezing lungs and aching legs.'

Looking at the Belchers' cottage from a lower level, seeing it on the horizon, it was obvious that the cottage was now a ruin. However, once Felicity had gained the top of the hill and was at the same level as the cottage, it gave the illusion of being whole again and as Felicity reached the boundary between the back garden of the cottage and the field, she realised that it was indeed whole again, that the cottage was not the burnt-out wreck it had been. For a moment she stood in utter confusion by the small gate, which gave direct access from the field into the garden. Had she mistaken the way, had she ended up at the wrong cottage? Then, with a thudding heart she suddenly realised that she must be seeing the cottage, not in real time anymore but before the fire. As the realization struck her, out of the corner of her eye, away to the left by the hedge she saw a movement. She shrank away from the gate, backing into the field and waited. A figure emerged from the camouflage of the hedge; the person was in a great hurry and was carrying a sizeable package. The speed with which the figure moved towards her almost made Felicity scream aloud; it looked as if she could not fail to be seen. Now within a few feet of her, the figure opened the gate and almost ran towards the house. The gate had been left open; Felicity followed through it. Her mouth was dry, she was scared to death, yet she strained her eyes, looking for any detail which might help. The figure was crouched now by the back door and suddenly the whole area was illuminated by flames coming from the parcel which he started to push through the cat flap. The flaming bundle appeared too big for the cat flap and the arsonist was having to push hard to get it through. Suddenly it gave way and dropped down into the house. There was a yelp of pain, a male voice she noted. In his efforts to force the blazing bundle into the house, the gloves on both hands were alight. He bashed his hands on the ground trying to extinguish the fire. This did no good and cursing under his breath he managed to pull one glove off and then the other. He doubled up in pain holding his hands tight to him, then gathered up the smouldering gloves and started running back towards the gate. At the gate he turned and faced the cottage; a good blaze was now established in the kitchen. Felicity, standing just a few yards from the figure, tried to see his face but in the dark it was quite impossible. Carefully he shut the gate behind him. Again there was some cursing under his breath; his hands were obviously very painful. Then with a final look at the house he was gone, back the way he came. He would be passing Keith Penrose who would now have started his journey up the hill, Felicity thought; at least he would have done if they'd been in the same time zone. She turned her attention back to the house; the flames were now six feet tall and gathering strength. She had the absurd desire to shout a warning to the Belchers, to find water to douse the flames, to run round to the front and get the door open and go in and rescue the children. She knew it was mad, she knew it was all too late. She closed her eyes. 'Those poor children.' Tears began pouring down her face: to have to watch it, to have to watch them die. She opened her eyes again and there was nothing, just the outline of the collapsed roof, the chimney brace standing alone; it was over, mercifully it was over and she wasn't going to have to see any more – a mother's desperate attempt to rescue her children, the screams – she had been spared that. She felt suddenly very tired and weak; it seemed a terrible effort to put one foot in front of the other. Slowly she made her way back to the gate. Below her in the field she could see a moving pinprick of light. She shut the gate with a resounding click.

'Felicity, is that you?' The disembodied voice of Keith Penrose came as a huge comfort.

'Yes,' she managed.

'Are you alright?'

'I think so.'

He was beside her in a few moments and ridiculously all that she could think of was that he appeared not to be out of breath at all. He was nearly ten years older than her; it was dreadful, she must get fit. The torch was shone on her face.

'You're crying,' he said, softly. 'You saw something?'

She nodded. 'Could we get away from here – somewhere, anywhere? I need to get away from here, sorry.'

'Are you alright to drive? I knew you should have let me pick you up.'

'I'm alright,' said Felicity.

'So where would you like to go?'

'Home,' she bleated.

They walked in silence from Barnoon Car Park, where they left their cars, down through the thread of little lanes which took them to Jericho Cottage. Once inside they headed straight for the kitchen.

'Coffee, wine?' Felicity managed her manners.

'I don't suppose you've got any whisky, have you?' Keith asked.

Felicity shook her head. 'I've got brandy.'

'Brandy and coffee then, thank you. Point me in the direction of the glasses and I'll fix us both a brandy.'

'I don't drink brandy,' Felicity began.

'You do tonight,' Keith said, firmly. They sat down with their drinks at the kitchen table and eyed one another cautiously. 'You look terrible,' Keith said.

'You have a wonderful way with words, Chief Inspector,' Felicity said.

'I'm not going to fire questions at you, just tell me what you saw in your own time.' And so she did. She told her story, a slight frown playing between her

80

eyes, as she concentrated hard on forgetting nothing, no detail. When she finished she took a sip of brandy, her hand trembled as she picked up the glass, but he'd been right; the fiery liquid was a comfort.

'I'm sorry to have put you through this,' he said, 'but some useful stuff has come out of it, hasn't it?'

'Well, he's a male, though I'd have thought that was pretty obvious. I can't imagine there have been many female arsonists.'

'No, I agree,' said Keith, 'so that cuts out half the population.'

'And he must have some quite bad burns to his hands. It took him a while to get those gloves off, enough time to create at least some damage. They were obviously painful, they won't have healed yet.'

'What sort of age do you put him at?'

Felicity thought hard. 'Well, he was quite fit, actually I'd say very fit, he moved very quickly. He was medium height, medium build I'm afraid, certainly not overweight but not slim either.' She eyed Keith with a slight smile. 'About your build, Chief Inspector, I would think, but taller.'

'He must have cut rather a dashing figure then,' Keith said, smiling back. 'What was he wearing?'

'Something dark, dark trousers, dark jumper or sweatshirt, no coat.'

'And his hair?'

'It was covered,' said Felicity, frowning, 'covered with a woolly hat, a beanie don't they call them, pulled right low over his face so that I couldn't really see anything much'

'And when he swore and cried out when he hurt his hands, what did he say?'

Felicity thought. 'I don't know,' she said, 'I'm really sorry. At first he just yelled out and then he sort of muttered under his breath, but what he said I've no idea.'

'And once he'd finished and he'd gone out through the gate, which way did he head?'

'Down towards you. If you'd been operating in the same time scale you'd have passed one another.'

Keith shuddered slightly. 'That statement makes me feel a bit odd,' he said, 'so heaven knows how it makes you feel.'

'I've sort of got used to it over the years,' Felicity said. 'I'm just so grateful ...' she hesitated.

'Grateful for what?' Keith asked.

'That I didn't have to see any more, that it faded. I didn't have to hear or see that poor little family die.'

Keith put out a hand and took hers. 'And I'm really, really grateful to you. I know this takes a terrible toll on you.'

'I'm not sure it's going to help much,' she smiled at him, 'but at least when you get your man, you'll know he should have burns on his hands.'

'Yes,' said Keith, 'and at least it puts David Belcher completely in the clear, not that he wasn't already. It won't stop my sergeant and the Super howling for his blood, though.'

'Will you tell them about tonight?'

'I'll tell Jack Curnow, my sergeant, he is almost a believer.'

'Really?' said Felicity.

'Yes, after you nailed Steve Jackson – that awful man who was pimping Eastern European girls, you remember?'

'I certainly do,' said Felicity.

'Well, then you'll remember you produced a credible drawing of Jackson before we'd even found him and arrested him. That really impressed young Jack so he'll certainly be looking for someone with burnt hands now.'

'Goodness,' said Felicity, 'I am flattered.'

'It is an extraordinary gift that you have. When we first met and you said that you'd seen your husband die, to be honest I thought you were a nutter.'

'Actually, Chief Inspector, as I recall you weren't particularly subtle about keeping your views to yourself.'

Keith laughed. 'Wasn't I?'

'No, you weren't, though up to a point, I do understand. I burst into your office telling you that you should be looking for someone I called 'the skunk' and I do appreciate it all sounded a bit far-fetched. To be honest after that little episode, I thought we'd never meet again and that I had completely wasted my time and yours.'

'Well there you go then,' said Keith, standing up. 'You go to bed right away, you look exhausted. Will you sleep alright?'

'I expect so,' said Felicity, 'though it's hard to get that cottage and what happened there out of one's head.'

Keith's expression was suddenly serious. 'I agree,' he said. 'Incidentally, I understand David Belcher was briefly your Mel's client?'

'Yes,' said Felicity. 'You should be grateful actually, she wanted me to plead with you on David Belcher's behalf but I refused. She was trying to help with gaining access to the children.'

'I know,' said Keith. 'When he was in custody Mel's senior partner, Arthur O'Sullivan, represented him and he mentioned Mel in case I wanted to talk to her.'

'And do you?'

'Not at the moment, we don't have a case as far as David Belcher is concerned.'

'What's her boss like, is he a nice chap?'

Keith shrugged. 'He's not someone you like meeting on the opposing side in court. He's clever, of course. I spend months tracking down some villain, finally get a case against him, know he's guilty as hell, get him before the judge and then Arthur O'Sullivan gets him off or gets him some ridiculously inappropriate sentence.'

'I suppose that's his job,' Felicity suggested.

'I suppose so,' said Keith, 'but talking of sleeping, I don't know how he sleeps at night sometimes.' He hesitated, frowning. 'I think what I'm saying is that for Arthur O'Sullivan the business of defending his client is like a game. For most lawyers the law itself is God and as far as possible it is the job of the court to ensure that those who have broken that law are dealt with appropriately. In Arthur's case there are no rights or wrongs, it's simply a question of winning. It's like he sat down to play backgammon or chess moving his evidence skilfully about so that he gets the result he wants, regardless of the rights or wrongs of the case.'

'He sounds like the sort of chap I'd like on my side if I ended up in court.'

'Oh yes, without a doubt,' Keith admitted, 'I just sometimes think he takes his zeal for defence too far.'

'I bet you wouldn't if it was you he was defending.'

Keith smiled. 'Good point. Anyway, to bed Mrs Paradise and thank you again.' He gave her one of his awkward hugs and thundered off down the stairs.

7

It was a long time since Felicity Paradise had been to a proper dinner party, not since her Oxford days and certainly she had never been to one before hosted by her daughter. Mel had pulled out all the stops, utterly refused any help and the result was impressive – crab paté, pheasant casserole and a delicious strawberry pavlova, the origins of which Mel made no attempt to keep secret.

'I've never been able to do this,' said Felicity, 'managed to keep the meringue moist.'

'Neither can I,' Mel admitted. 'In fact, I can't even make meringue at all, but I know someone who can.'

'Annie?' Felicity ventured.

'Exactly,' said Mel. 'I'll bring in some cheese. Martin, could you fetch the port?'

'This has been a veritable feast,' said Arthur O'Sullivan, clearly guest of honour.

Strangely, it had not been Mel's idea to wine and dine her boss. The idea of the dinner party had begun with Martin's request to invite some valuable customers. A couple from the Midlands were setting up a tea garden and were spending an absolute fortune with him – not only were they his best-ever customers but they were also a nice couple. Pete and Anne Turner, who ran a pottery in Hayle, had been roped in and then Mel had dreamed up the idea of including her boss and if her boss was to come then Felicity was needed to make up numbers. It was an interesting mix of people and the conversation flowed easily all evening, fuelled by plenty of wine. Mel and Martin made relaxed but efficient and attentive hosts which pleased Felicity, imagining how this ritual would develop and repeat itself over the years, like her and Charlie, she thought wistfully. In the end entertaining for them had become a seamless partnership which they had both adored.

'So where are you?' The deep voice of Arthur O'Sullivan cut through her thoughts and she looked up quickly and apologetically.

'I'm sorry.' The room had cleared apart from the two of them.

'Come through for coffee when you're ready and do refill your glasses,' Mel called as she left the room.

Felicity chewed on her lip thoughtfully. She was not a great one for confidences but she liked Arthur O'Sullivan instinctively and after so many years of Charlie and his colleagues she felt comfortable with a lawyer.

'Actually, I was thinking about my husband and

how we used to entertain such a lot. We were a good team and I was thinking Mel and Martin make a good team too. I suppose I was feeling a little wistful.'

'Mel probably told you that I'm widowed, too.' Felicity nodded. 'My wife has been dead nearly ten years now, but I still feel half of a whole.'

'Me too,' she said, 'I thought it would fade but it doesn't seem to.'

'You get used to it and there are compensations – like that girl of yours, you must be very proud of her.'

'I am,' said Felicity. 'She's getting on alright, is she?'

'She certainly is,' said Arthur. 'Reorganising the entire office, of course, bossing everybody about but she's extremely competent. I'm extremely pleased to have her on my side. Do you work, Mrs Paradise?'

'No, not really,' said Felicity, 'not proper work. I illustrate books, dabble in a bit of painting and work one day a week in the primary school in St Ives teaching art, but I have too much fun there to call it work.'

Arthur O'Sullivan laughed. He was an attractive man and very different from Charlie with dark neatly-cut hair going attractively white at the temples, as opposed to Charlie's white blonde unruly mop. He was trimmer and fitter-looking than poor Charlie had ever been. Felicity liked his smile and his laughter was infectious.

'Mel tells me you're a friend of Chief Inspector Penrose,' Arthur said, sipping his wine and studying

Felicity over the top of his glass.

'Yes, I am,' said Felicity.

'We're old sparring partners,' said Arthur, 'always on the opposite side in court, of course. A nice man but not tough enough for the job in my opinion.'

Felicity was immediately up in arms. 'I think he's a splendid policeman,' she said, angrily. 'Just because he's not aggressive and loutish doesn't mean he's not good at his job. He's very successful at solving cases, he just has his own way of doing things.'

'Whoa,' said Arthur, 'sorry, I've clearly touched a nerve. You really are a fan of his, aren't you?'

Felicity met his eye squarely. 'Yes,' she said, 'he's been a tremendous help to me, particularly around the time my husband died.'

'Was it from cancer, do you mind me asking, like my wife?'

'No,' said Felicity, 'no, he was knocked down by a car while biking home from work. It was a hit-and-run.' What she failed to add was that, in effect, it was murder. She knew it, Keith Penrose knew it, but there was no point in ever trying to prove it. There was a silence between them for a moment.

'What an awful shock,' said Arthur. 'My poor wife, Diana, fought cancer bravely for four years but I did at least have the chance to get used to the idea of her not being around. To lose your husband so suddenly like that must have been terrible.'

'It was,' said Felicity, 'and to be honest it still is.' She stood up abruptly, anxious not to betray her feelings. 'Shall we join the others?' she said.

Over coffee, the conversation veered towards the coming season. Felicity, happy to let others do the talking, listened with interest to the various views on the weather, last year's weather, the competition on offer from ludicrously cheap holiday deals abroad, the huge cost of holidaying in the UK … the season touched everyone in West Cornwall, she thought. A good season meant that the little businesses supporting families all over the Duchy would survive another winter; a poor season meant untold hardship, the economy was so fragile.

'These arson attacks don't help,' Arthur said to no one in particular.

'I agree,' said Martin, 'I was in the post office the other morning and there was a lot of chatter and speculation as to who would be next. It makes everyone nervous, particularly after what happened to that poor little family.'

'Someone told me they were clients of yours, is that right?' Pete, the potter, asked Mel.

Mel glanced at Arthur, client confidentiality clearly on her mind. He answered for both of them. 'No,' he said, 'the father of the family, David Belcher, is a client of ours but he was in no way involved in the fire.'

'I thought he was arrested,' persisted Pete.

'No,' said Arthur, smoothly, 'he was taken in for questioning, obviously because it was his family who had died but there was no question of our client being involved; not that we should be talking about it,' he said, cleverly concluding the conversation.

'The press always get it wrong,' Martin added helpfully.

'Let's just hope the story doesn't go national,' Felicity said, echoing Keith's sentiments.

'I doubt there'll be time for that,' said Arthur with a mischievous grin, 'according to Mrs Paradise, Keith Penrose will be arresting the villain any day now.'

'You don't like him, do you?' Felicity challenged Arthur, who had offered to drive her home after the party. She had accepted rather ungraciously; she was not at all sure she liked this man.

'Keith? I don't dislike him, I just find him rather a bore. He takes himself and his job rather too seriously for my liking, that's all. Anyway let's not talk about the good Chief Inspector anymore, since we're bound to disagree. I was wondering whether you'd care to have dinner with me next week.'

Felicity was flummoxed. 'I'm not sure,' she said.

'Look I'm not trying to make a big deal out of this.'

They were dropping down into St Ives. The harbour came into view; it was a still quiet night, pinpricks of light reflecting onto the water – a magical place.

'No, I'm sure you're not,' Felicity answered.

'Damn,' said Arthur, 'I'm doing this rather badly. I haven't asked a woman out for a very long time. Where do you want me to drop you incidentally?'

'Oh, just drive along the Wharf, outside the Sloop would be fine.' There was an awkward silence between them as Arthur stopped the car opposite the Sloop.

'So will you?' he asked.

What the hell, Felicity thought, an attractive man asking me out for dinner; Mel's boss too, it wouldn't be a good idea to upset him. Mind made up, she turned to him.

'I'd be delighted,' she said, graciously.

Chief Inspector Keith Penrose was making a valiant effort to tidy his office. This was something which normally only occurred at the completion of a case but the arson attacks had created so much paperwork that even he realised that there needed to be some order brought to the chaos. He picked up his notes relating to the death of the little boy in the Hayle Estuary. That one's for the shredder, he thought. It was a complete red herring, poor little chap. He opened the file and read what he had written during his interview with Martin Tregonning. There really is nothing here, he thought as he leafed through the details. Then, suddenly, the names of the family jumped out at him. The children, Jake and Daisy Jones, the parents Theresa and Harry. Harry – Harry Jones; that was the name of Mrs Belcher's boyfriend, the vending machine salesman. Surely they couldn't be one and the same? It was not an unusual name, and yet at the merest thought of such a possibility, he was round the desk and out of his office door in a moment. 'Jack!' he shouted down the corridor.

He was lucky with his sergeant, Keith thought, glancing at his watch. In a little under two hours, Jack had established that Harry Jones of the Hayle tragedy and Harry Jones, boyfriend of Mrs Belcher, were indeed one and the same and that Harry was to be found, having checked with the company for which he worked, in the Gweek Inn. So here he was sitting opposite Keith, impatient and obviously ill at ease.

'I've already been interviewed about the arson attack,' he said, 'it was a real personal tragedy for me, you know. I loved that woman and those little children like my own. You should be respecting my feelings and leave me alone to grieve.'

'You did have two children of your own,' said Keith, ignoring his protestations. The expression on Harry Jones's face darkened. Keith could see why he was a success with women. He was tall, dark, good-looking, but he had a weak, greedy face. Keith didn't like him at all.

'Yes,' Harry stammered slightly, 'yes, that's right.'

'And your son, Jake, died in the Hayle Estuary before the air sea rescue helicopter could save him?'

'Why bring that up?' Harry Jones snarled at Keith. He'd raised his voice, causing one or two lunchtime drinkers at the bar to turn and stare at the two men.

'Were you satisfied with the way Culdrose handled the rescue?'

'There shouldn't have needed to be a rescue,' Harry hissed. 'Theresa, the daft cow, just sat there like a lump of lard while the children were swept out to sea, it's unbelievable.'

'I take it you and your wife are no longer together?' Keith asked mildly.

'We separated soon after the accident, after a few weeks. I just couldn't stand the sight of her, after what she'd done.'

'That must have been hard for your daughter.'

'No, she's like her mother. Thick as thieves those two, they don't need me around.'

'So, judging by what you've said,' Keith said, 'you blame your wife for the accident, not Culdrose.'

'Of course it was her fault, stupid bitch.'

'And where were you when the accident happened?' Keith asked. He really did dislike this man.

'I went up the car park, I couldn't get a signal down on the beach and I needed to make a phone call.'

'About work?'

Harry had the grace to look uncomfortable. 'Actually I was phoning this friend of mine, it took rather longer than I expected.'

'A woman I assume?' Keith said. Harry didn't

disagree. 'And by the time you got back it was too late?'

'Yes,' he said, 'when I got back Theresa was still sitting on the beach reading a magazine, would you believe, and the children were just a dot on the horizon. I had to run back up again to get a signal to dial 999. The lifeguard chap was there very quickly.'

'And did you feel he did a good job?'

Harry nodded. 'Yes, of course, he did his best, he saved Daisy, didn't he? Why are you asking all these questions?'

Keith took his time in replying. 'Whoever is responsible for these arson attacks, including the tragic deaths of Mrs Belcher and her children, we believe had some grudge against Culdrose. It just occurred to me to be rather an odd coincidence that you should have lost a child during a Culdrose rescue attempt and also had a really close association with the Belcher family.'

'Coincidence is the right word,' Harry replied, belligerently. 'You can't pin this one on me, Chief Inspector, you know where I was – one hundred and fifty miles away and there are witnesses.'

Keith nodded. 'I know where you were on the evening of the fire but the attack happened in the early hours of the morning. You'd have had plenty of time to drive down here.'

'But I stayed the night at a B & B, you've checked that out. This is police harassment.'

'It's not,' said Keith, fighting his rising temper.

'If you really profess to have cared for the Belcher family as you say you do, then you'd be doing everything in your power to help me find who was responsible for their deaths.'

Harry appeared totally unmoved. 'Have you anything else to ask me, only I have to get on. I have a job to do, you know?'

'No,' said Keith, heavily, 'you get off.' Harry stood up and turned away from him. 'Oh, just one thing,' said Keith.

'What now?' said Harry.

'Could I see your hands?'

'What, why?'

'Indulge me,' said Keith.

Harry held out his hands. Like the rest of him, they were very well groomed, a perfect manicure, smooth hands almost like a woman's, but totally unscarred.

'Thank you, Mr Jones, that will be all.'

'You're going on a hot date with my boss? Honestly Mother, if you have to go out with a man, couldn't you choose someone slightly further away from home, certainly no one associated with me?'

Felicity was sitting at Mel's kitchen table with Minty on her lap. 'I'm not a leper,' she said, not unreasonably.

'I'm not saying you are.' Mel was crashing pans about on the stove. 'I'm just saying it's awkward. Supposing he went and fell for you or something – yuck.'

'Oh thanks,' said Felicity. 'You're making me feel better by the moment. I'm just having dinner with him, Mel, I don't even especially like him.'

'Then why didn't you just say no?'

'Because if I'd have said no I thought it would have been rude and I didn't want to do anything to upset him, given that he's your boss. I was trying to be helpful.'

'You're always helpful,' said Martin, coming into the room. 'What's all this about – a mother and daughter dispute, I sense?'

'Mum's accepted an invitation to go out to dinner with Arthur O'Sullivan, can you believe it?' said Mel.

'Really?' Martin beamed at Felicity. 'That's great, at last. It's about time you started having some fun.'

'It's just dinner,' Felicity protested.

'I should hope so,' said Mel. 'Mother dating, it's gross, I might have to go and throw up.'

'I gather you're having dinner with Arthur O'Sullivan.' Keith was standing in the field behind the Belchers' house, mobile in hand, staring yet again at the burnt-out wreck of a cottage, desperate for inspiration.

'Chief Inspector, I don't know where you get your information but it feels like you're checking up on me,' Felicity replied.

'He told me, with some considerable glee, I might add. We bumped into each other in court yesterday. He described you as a charming woman.'

'I am a charming woman,' said Felicity, 'and there's absolutely no reason for you to be grumpy about it. You're as bad as Mel.'

'He's a snake,' said Keith. 'I don't like the chap, you be careful. Mel's quite right. She must know him pretty well as he's her boss, you should listen to what she has to say.'

'Honestly,' said Felicity, 'I'm fifty, Keith, I'm hardly a teenager out on my first date. You and Mel are being absolutely ridiculous, at least Martin is pleased for me.'

'Really,' said Keith, 'I always thought Martin Tregonning was a sensible sort of chap. I'm clearly going to have to reconsider my opinion.'

Arthur took her to Porthminster Beach Café which was Felicity's absolute favourite place. It was a beautiful, calm evening and they had opted to sit outside, and in the gathering dusk the view across the bay to the Island was stunning. The waitress had provided them with rugs for their knees to keep them warm and they were drinking champagne – it was idyllic.

'Why champagne?' Felicity asked, 'It's lovely but are we celebrating something?'

Arthur smiled at her. 'Well I certainly am,' he said. 'It's a very long time since I took a beautiful woman out for a meal.'

'Please,' said Felicity, 'I'm not good with flattery and in any case, I don't believe you haven't taken anyone out since your wife died.'

'I wine and dine clients and work colleagues and my daughter when she deigns to come and visit the old man, but otherwise I live a positively monastic life these days. What about you?'

'The same,' Felicity admitted. 'I'm very involved with my family, I have three grandchildren, including my little granddaughter. Thanks to you and your job offer to Mel, looing after Minty is a permanent commitment now.'

'Mel was ready to come back to work,' Arthur said.

'I don't disagree with you and I am enjoying looking after Minty,' said Felicity. 'It wasn't a moan, just an observation. I have friends in Cornwall and friends in Oxford, none of whom I see often enough – life is very full really.'

'But no partner to share it with?'

'No,' said Felicity.

'Are you ready to move on?' Arthur said. 'Forgive me, this isn't some embarrassing play for your affections, I'm just genuinely interested in whether you feel you can move forward from your husband's death as yet.'

'I don't know,' said Felicity, 'I try not to think about it, just do the one day at a time thing.'

'You're far too young to be alone for the rest of your life.'

'So everyone keeps telling me,' said Felicity, 'that and how I've got to be careful about going out with you.'

Arthur took a sip of his champagne. 'Really, so you've been warned off me, have you? By whom?'

Felicity cursed herself; obviously she couldn't quote Mel's feelings on the subject so that only left Keith to blame.

'Chief Inspector Penrose.'

'Oh him,' said Arthur dismissively. 'He's just jealous.'

'Hardly,' said Felicity, 'he's a happily married man and a very moral one.'

'Then you'll just have to take my word for it,' said Arthur. 'In my view he'd give anything to be in my shoes right now.'

In fact Arthur O'Sullivan was completely right. At that precise moment Keith Penrose was sitting in his car in a lay-by on the A30. His wife Barbara had called. She and their son Will had just had a shouting match, ending with Will storming out of the house.

'I'm not going to be shouted at in my own home, Keith,' Barbara had said. 'The boy's out of control. I tell you I've had enough, it's either him or me. I've asked you and asked you to speak to him and find out what's going on and what do you do, nothing! Work, of course, the pressure of work, the same old excuse over and over again. If you had been here for him when he was a little boy …'

'Yes, yes,' said Keith, wearily. 'But I can't see any point in talking to him tonight. By the time he comes home, assuming he does come home, he'll be drunk and we'll get no sense out of him at all.'

'Alright,' said Barbara, 'well then you'll just have to stay home in the morning and talk to him then.'

'I can't do that,' said Keith, patiently. 'I've got a nine o'clock appointment with the boss.'

'You'll have to do something, Keith,' said Barbara. 'If you don't sort him out, I'm going to pack my bags and move into a hotel. It's him or me.'

'We can't just throw him out, Barbara,' said Keith. 'He's our son. Obviously something has gone wrong with his Army career or he wouldn't be here, back with us. He's obviously very upset and angry about something.'

'Then it's time we found out what,' said Barbara. 'You've always been too soft on the boy, Keith, you really have and now I'm suffering from the consequences because, as usual, you're never here.'

Keith hadn't smoked for over thirty years but sitting morosely in the car after the exchange he suddenly longed for a cigarette to calm his nerves. Family confrontations were his worst form of torture. He glanced at his watch: seven-forty-five. It was time he went home and faced the music. Reluctantly, he started the engine of the car. Seven-forty-five – tonight was the night Felicity was going out with Arthur O'Sullivan. What on earth had possessed her to spend time with that man, he wondered? He would have thought she'd have had more sense. He pulled out into the stream of traffic. Still, her husband had been a lawyer; maybe she felt comfortable with the legal profession – but Arthur O'Sullivan! Hopefully their dinner together would be a one-off.

The dog lay in his usual place but his skull was smashed open and the gaping wound behind his ear oozed with blood. 'Things were much easier now this was done,' the old man thought. He and the dog had been so close, thought the same thoughts, felt the same feelings. The dog had known all day what lay ahead of him. He had not been afraid, he had trusted his master as he had always done. It had been a magical evening, one of those clear skies where the stars and moon are up before the light from the sun has quite gone. Man and dog had said goodbye to the world on the hillock just outside the cottage. Gazing about them, smelling the flowers, the dog pricking up his ears at a rustle in the undergrowth – a rat, a rabbit? His arthritic joints made further investigation impossible. The man had fed the dog, as usual, though the dog had not touched his food and instead had lain down on his rug and waited. The man had poured himself a whisky and with an unsteady hand had loaded his shotgun. Even when he put the muzzle of the gun to the dog's head the dog neither stirred nor flinched, just accepted his fate.

The old man gazed around his cottage, his eyes as always settling on the photograph of the little girl. 'Not long now, pet,' he said.

He would have liked to have died like his dog, a single shot, but killing himself with a shotgun was not easy, the barrel was just too long. During the last few weeks he'd first devised and then discarded a variety of schemes from sawing down the barrel to using various objects to pull the trigger but none of them was foolproof. He didn't want to die a slow agonising death, he wanted to go cleanly like his dog. He picked up the coil of rope he had brought into the cottage earlier in the day. He placed the kitchen chair in the middle of the room and unsteadily climbed onto it. It was difficult raising his arms above his head, they ached so, but with a huge effort he threw the rope and on the second attempt it went over the beam. He grunted with satisfaction. He tied one end of the rope to the leg of the old Cornish range – he was a slight man so it could bear his weight – the other end he turned into a slipknot. He downed the remains of his whisky and without any hesitation climbed back onto the rickety chair, slipped the noose over his neck, let the rope take his weight and kicked away the chair. 'I'm coming, pet,' was his last thought.

It was surprising how little it hurt as the life slowly choked out of him. All he really felt was a profound sense of relief.

8

The evening was proving most unproductive for the Penrose family. Barbara had a shepherd's pie waiting when Keith reluctantly crossed the threshold. There was no sign of their son.

'I'm not sitting up all night waiting to talk to him when he'll probably be incoherent anyway,' Keith said, without preamble.

'I agree,' said Barbara, surprisingly, 'but now I've got you here, it is a good opportunity for us to talk about him, Keith. We can't just pretend this isn't happening. Something is terribly wrong with the boy and we need to get to the bottom of it.'

'He's not a boy, he's a man,' said Keith. 'He needs to make his own mistakes, find his own path through life. We can't keep mollycoddling him all the time.'

'Would you like a beer or a glass of wine?' Barbara asked.

'Wine, please.'

They settled down at the table with glasses of red wine. Keith wasn't hungry but made a valiant attempt at his shepherd's pie. He recognised that Barbara was stretching out a hand of friendship, trying to make up for the harsh words she had spoken earlier. He needed to meet her halfway and he knew, of course, that she was right, something needed to be done.

'He's got this friend,' said Barbara, 'I don't know if you've heard much about him.'

Keith shook his head.

'His name's Nick, he was in the Army too, same regiment as Billy.'

'Will,' Keith corrected.

'He'll always be my Billy boy,' said Barbara, smiling slightly.

Keith reached out and patted her arm. 'That's half the trouble, love, isn't it?'

'Probably,' Barbara acknowledged. 'Anyway, this friend Nick, he's older than Will, about ten years I think.'

'Have you met him?' Keith asked.

'No, I've seen him. He has a car and comes to pick up Will sometimes. He looks alright, still got his short Army hair.'

'What sort of car does he drive?' Keith asked.

'I don't believe it,' said Barbara. 'What a typical male question that is! We're supposed to be talking about whether he's a good influence on our son and all you can think about is the type of car he drives!'

'It could have a bearing,' said Keith. 'Cars, like dogs, often give an insight into the character of their owner.'

'Well it's blue,' said Barbara, 'dark blue, almost navy.'

Keith chuckled and took a sip of wine. 'And that's it?' he said.

'Yes,' said Barbara, defensively.

'Typical female reaction, if I may say so. Blue, for heaven's sake! Thank God it's me who's the policeman in this family.'

'Stop it, Keith, this is serious.'

'I know, I know,' said Keith. 'What time does Will get up in the mornings?'

'I don't know,' said Barbara, 'certainly after you and I have gone to work.'

'My meeting with the Super is at the station and it's not going to take very long. What will happen is that I am going to be given the most almighty bollocking for not having solved the arson cases and be threatened with everything under the sun. I can't see it taking more than ten minutes. I should be back here by nine-thirty, nine-forty-five at the worst. I could talk to him then.'

'And I haven't got a meeting until after lunch tomorrow,' said Barbara. 'Would you like me to go into work late and be here when you talk to him?'

Keith stared at his cooling plate of shepherd's pie. 'Yes, I would rather,' he said.

'You're hopeless,' said Barbara, but her voice was affectionate.

'I know,' Keith agreed. 'Perhaps we'd better find out more about this friend.'

'Yes, I think we should try,' said Barbara. 'I don't know anything about him, not even his surname, but the two of them seem to be thick as thieves.'

'So it's definitely Nick who Will goes drinking with every night. What does Carly think?' Keith asked.

'She's as much in the dark as we are. She tried to take Will out for dinner last week but he wouldn't come, said he was too busy.'

'Busy!' said Keith. 'I must say, I wouldn't mind some of his sort of busy.'

'Have you thought about that?' Barbara asked.

'What?' Keith looked up from his plate, abandoning his fork and all attempts at eating any more.

'Retirement, Keith, it's not long off now.'

'I can't say I have,' Keith said.

'Only nowadays they will allow me to work on for three or four more years after my retirement date,' said Barbara, 'and we've got to decide whether I should or shouldn't and what you want to do, whether you want to travel or some such. Most people do something on retirement.'

'I can't think about it at the moment,' said Keith.

'Well you'll have to sometime.'

Keith smiled at her. 'Not necessarily, the way the Super feels about me right now, I may not last until retirement.'

'A second date!' In common with all parents of

very small children, Mel tended to think of half-past-seven in the morning as halfway through the day. Felicity was only just out of her bath.

'It's not a date exactly, Mel. It's just that he gave me a very nice dinner at Porthminster and it seemed churlish not to invite him back.'

'Invite him back? You mean he's coming to your cottage?'

'Yes, next week for supper.'

'Mother, you're a bit old for this sort of thing, aren't you? Not to mention Arthur, he's even older, *and* he's my boss – surely you can find someone else.'

'It's not a question of finding anybody,' Felicity said, tartly. 'For heaven's sake, Mel, you're blowing the whole thing out of proportion. He asked me out for supper, I've asked him back. OK, so he's a widower and I'm alone too, but that doesn't mean romance is in the air. We're a couple of mature people who enjoy each other's company and that's all there is to it, right?'

'Right,' said Mel, reluctantly.

Superintendent George Stapleton always cut an imposing figure. He was a big man in every sense of the word; in height, in girth, in breadth of shoulder; and when he was angry, he seemed to be huge. Normally he had a very high regard for Keith Penrose but he was starting to wonder whether the man was losing his grip. Keith had just finished a brave but utterly fruitless speech about the progress he and his team were making in the hunt for the arsonist.

'In other words, Keith,' said George, dryly, 'you've made absolutely no progress. It isn't the father, it isn't the boyfriend, and you've no other leads.'

'Well, we know the common denominator,' said Keith, clutching at straws, 'we know the link is Culdrose, we just don't know why.'

'Culdrose could very easily be a red herring,' said George. 'It's not too much of a stretch of the imagination to see the link to Culdrose being nothing more than a coincidence. The tentacles from the Base stretch far and wide across West Cornwall. You could probably pick a dozen people off the street and find that they had some connection with Culdrose if you dug deep enough.'

'I disagree, sir,' said Keith, bravely.

'Well then, for God's sake, Keith, prove your point! This situation is like a tinderbox. I'm managing to sit on the local press at the moment to keep the story low-key because the locals understand how damaging this could be for the season, but any moment now a national is going to pick it up – a mother and her three tiny children burnt to death after a string of arson attacks – it's very newsworthy.'

Keith winced.

'Come to sunny Cornwall where an arsonist is still on the loose after five successful fires. What a fantastic place to bring a young family on holiday!' The sarcasm in George's voice was heavy. He stood up and loomed over Keith. 'Do you think the job is getting too much for you, Keith? I know you've had all this trouble with your daughter. How is she, by the way?'

'No, the job is not getting too much for me, sir, thank you,' Keith said, 'and my daughter is fine, in remission, has been now for over a year.'

'Excellent, excellent,' said George, wandering over to the window. In the silence that followed, Keith's mobile rang.

'Do you mind if I take it, sir?'

'No, go ahead,' said George.

It was Barbara. 'Keith, Billy didn't come home last night.'

'Not now Barbara, I'm in a meeting.'

'I'm so worried, do you think he's left home?'

'Barbara, I'll call you back.' Keith turned off his mobile. 'Sorry about that, sir.'

'Trouble with the missus?' George turned from the window.

Keith shook his head. 'No sir, I just promised I'd pop home during the day and talk to our son.' Damn his honesty, Keith thought under his breath. He should have made something up.

George frowned. 'Your son, Billy, isn't it?'

Keith nodded.

'He's in the Army, I thought.'

'He's left the Army now, he's just come back home.'

'Has he now?' said George. 'Well the Army is a very good training for the Force. Do you think you can get him to follow in his father's footsteps?'

'I'm not sure …' Keith hesitated.

'Is something wrong with the boy?'

'He seems a bit unstable at the moment, difficult to talk to.'

'Well I'm sorry to hear that Keith, but I hope you're not letting your trouble at home overshadow the importance of solving this case.'

Keith was suddenly very angry. 'When have I ever put my family before my job?' he said, rising to his feet. 'Never! Maybe that's half the trouble, maybe I should have done so now and again; and as for my mind not being on this case, if you'd seen the bodies of those little children!' The image of the children came into his mind and he stopped, the anger draining away from him. 'I'm sorry, but I really resent the idea that I might not be giving this case my full attention.'

'Then for Christ's sake, Keith,' George exploded, 'get a bloody result.'

'He's not here, hasn't been all night.' Barbara said. She'd been waiting anxiously for Keith in the kitchen.

Keith shrugged his shoulders and headed for the electric kettle. 'So, he's stayed with a mate, he'll turn up when he's good and ready, no doubt.'

'I just hope he's alright,' said Barbara.

'Oh, Barbara, for goodness sake!' said Keith. 'He's been on tour in Iraq, in Afghanistan – how can you compare that to a night out in Truro?'

Barbara turned away from her husband. 'I told him to go,' she said. From the dejected set of his wife's shoulders, Keith suddenly realised she was terribly upset.

His voice softened. 'What do you mean, love?'

'I told him that if he couldn't pull himself together and at least talk to us and tell us what was going on, and if he couldn't get a job and didn't lay off the booze, he wasn't welcome here any more.'

Keith crossed the kitchen, turned Barbara around and took her in his arms.

'You said what was right. Has he taken his stuff then?'

'No, no,' said Barbara, 'all his things are still here, he just slammed his way out of the house. I never thought I'd ever tell a child of mine that they weren't welcome in our home, it's terrible. I shouldn't have done it, not without understanding first what's wrong with him, what's happened. This should be his haven, this is where he belongs and I told him to go.'

'He's not a child, Barbara.' Keith stroked her back. 'He's seen enough of the world to realise that there was no depth to your words, you just reacted to his bad behaviour. He knows we're always here for him, always have been always will be.'

Barbara drew away from her husband's embrace. 'You don't get it, Keith, do you?'

Keith frowned. 'Get what?'

'I'm not regretting that I gave Will a good

talking-to, he deserved it. What I mind is that I had to do it at all.'

'What do you mean?' Keith asked.

'It shouldn't be me sorting him out, it should have been his father.'

9

By the time Keith reached his desk, he was in a very unreceptive mood. To have been lectured both by his boss and his wife all in one morning was too much. He glanced at his watch; it wasn't even eleven o'clock – a great start to the day! What made it worse was that he knew they were both justified in their criticism of him; he should have cracked the arson case by now and, of course, he should have talked to his son. This knowledge only heightened his ill temper so when Jack put his head around the door, whatever he had to say would have been met with a negative response.

'Sir, I need you to come with me, we've a suicide out on the Lizard, we're needed at the scene now.'

'Who is it?' Keith asked.

'It's an old boy, a farmer, hanged himself, shot his dog.'

'Other way around, I imagine,' said Keith. Jack frowned. 'Well, shot his dog and then hung himself.'

'It's not funny, he was a neighbour of ours.'

Keith let out a sigh and stood up. 'I'm so sorry Jack, I've just had a bit of a morning. That's awful, someone close to you?'

'Close to my parents. It's rather a long story, he's had a very hard life and my parents kind of looked out for him. He used to have Sunday lunch with us most weeks.'

Keith hesitated. 'Jack, I don't wish to sound callous, but sadly your friend isn't the first farmer to have committed suicide. I'm up to my neck here trying to sort out this arson case. If you need some support to visit the scene and you feel you need to go, then maybe your father could accompany you. I presume the case is being handled at Helston?'

'It's not that, sir,' said Jack, patiently. 'I think his death could have a bearing on the arson case.'

'Why would that be?' said Keith.

'Can I explain it to you in the car? I really think we should go out there and take a look.'

Suddenly the thought of sitting at his desk, uselessly pushing pieces of paper around, held little appeal compared with getting out of this office. Even if it was a wild goose chase, it would be better than nothing.

'Right,' said Keith, 'I'll take your word for it. Let's go.'

Felicity was sitting at Annie's kitchen table recording for posterity Annie's fish pie recipe, complete with its wonderful crumble topping.

'I ought to write down all your recipes,' said Felicity.

'Yes,' said Annie, 'we could turn them into a book and you could illustrate it.'

'It's not such a stupid idea,' said Felicity.

'Maybe,' said Annie. She cocked her head on one side and regarded Felicity for a moment. 'So what's this fish pie in aid of?'

'I've someone coming for supper,' Felicity said.

'What sort of someone?' Annie asked.

'A friend.'

'Aah,' said Annie, 'a man.'

'What on earth makes you think that?' Felicity asked, immediately on the defensive.

'Because you're being secretive about it, my girl. That must mean he's a potential boyfriend.'

'Hardly a boyfriend, Annie dear,' Felicity said, 'he must be nearer sixty than fifty.'

'Right,' said Annie, 'I'm not giving you the rest of that recipe until you tell me all about him.'

'That's blackmail,' said Felicity.

'Yes,' Annie said, with a triumphant grin. Five minutes later she had all the details of Arthur O'Sullivan. 'He sounds just right, my girl, but what's the problem? I sense there is one?'

'Trust you, Annie,' said Felicity. 'Only my daughter and Chief Inspector Penrose.'

'Good Lord, what have they got to do with it?'

'Well, Arthur O'Sullivan is Mel's boss and she doesn't like me seeing him. I can understand that.'

'Don't see why,' said Annie, 'and what about your Inspector, what's he got against him?'

'He doesn't like him, he says he's a snake.'

'How do they know each other?' Annie asked.

'They meet in court. Poor old Keith gets the villains to the courtroom door and then Arthur defends them and tries to get them off.'

'Well, there are two explanations for your inspector's attitude,' said Annie. 'One is the reason he's given, the other is he's jealous.'

'Don't be silly,' said Felicity, 'of course he's not jealous, he's a married man.'

'He's very fond of you, that inspector.'

'You're talking absolute rubbish, Annie.'

'We'll see won't we, my lover.'

'I've arranged for my father to be at the scene.' Jack said, as he took the Falmouth road out of Truro. 'I've also told forensics not to move the body until you've seen it.'

'Good, thanks,' said Keith. 'Now are you going to tell me what this is all about, Jack?'

'The old boy who killed himself was called Tom Lawson. His farm adjoins my parents' farm. Tom was married and had three children, two boys and a girl, all older than me, I never knew them but my sister and my older brother used to play with them, apparently.'

'Go on,' said Keith.

'It must have been about thirty years ago – Dad

can tell you the exact date – there was an accident, a helicopter taking off from Culdrose Air Base crashed. No one ever knew what happened, it was a perfect day apparently, the pilot and co-pilot were very experienced and obviously tried valiantly to put down somewhere which would cause minimum risk to the public.'

'So where did it come down?' said Keith.

'On an old barn on Tom Lawson's farm. The barn was stacked full of straw, the helicopter exploded on impact and of course the resulting fire was huge, the hay acting as fuel.'

'At least it didn't crash on the farmhouse,' Keith said.

'Two of the Lawson children were in the barn at the time,' Jack said quietly. Their car was stationary waiting in a queue at the Penryn roundabout. The silence made Jack glance across at his boss. 'Did you hear what I said, sir?'

'I did,' said Keith. 'Are you suggesting that this old boy, Tom Lawson, is the man who might have been taking revenge for the killing of his children?'

'I've been thinking of nothing else since I heard the news,' said Jack. The traffic was moving; he negotiated his way around the roundabout.

'And?' Keith asked.

'And I can't see it. The tragedy didn't end with the deaths of the two children. Tom's wife never got over their deaths. There was a baby still at home, and after a few months, she and the baby took off and Tom never saw them again.'

'What, not even the child?'

'No. My parents used to try to persuade him to trace them. It wouldn't have been difficult but he said that if his wife needed a clean break, then that's the least he could do for her – she'd suffered so much losing her children.'

'He'd suffered too,' Keith suggested.

'I know,' said Jack, 'but that rather sums him up, I think. He was not a man who found dealing with people very easy. The extent of any conversation I ever had with him was regarding the weather.'

'Mrs Paradise maintains that arsonists are usually loners,' Keith said.

'He was an old man,' Jack said, 'it's why I've asked Dad to join us, because he knew him so well, but when I suggested the idea to Dad about him being an arsonist, he laughed; "Old Tom wouldn't hurt a fly" he said.'

'Well, we'll see won't we,' said Keith.

The farm looked like something from another century, the yard caked in mud, the barn doors hanging loose, the adjacent cottage appeared about ready to fall down.

'Poor old chap,' said Keith, as the two men climbed out of the car, 'he can't have had many creature comforts.'

'There was a farmhouse where the family lived before the accident about a quarter of a mile further down the track. After the tragedy Old Tom sold it, once his wife and baby left him. The National Trust bought it and turned it into a holiday let. He was a good farmer once.' They nodded at the young constable standing by the front door and ducking low went into the dark interior of the cottage. Dr Horace Greenaway was just leaving.

'Ah, Penrose, I was told you were on your way. This isn't your patch, what's your interest? It seems a pretty straightforward case to me.'

Keith ignored the question and looked down at the body which had been cut from the rope and was now lying on the ground close beside the dog – it was a bleak scene.

'So what do you think we've got here then?' he asked Horace.

'Pretty obvious – another exhausted, dispirited farmer living alone topped himself, poor chap. Clearly devoted to his dog and made sure the dog didn't suffer without him – end of story, nothing sinister. He used the weight of the range to secure the rope, which was sensible.'

'Sensible?' Keith said.

'Well, made sure he did a good job. No point in trying to hang yourself unless you do it properly.'

'You're a weird one, Horace,' Keith said affectionately.

'Well, are you surprised in my job? Any questions before I go?'

'Just the one,' said Keith. 'Was there any injury

to his hands?'

Horace frowned and returned to the body.

'None that I noticed,' he said crouching low. He picked up first one old, calloused, deeply-veined hand. 'No.' He picked up the other. 'They tell a story these hands, years of toil in all weathers, but there's no injury. What were you looking for?'

'I'm not sure,' said Keith, evasively.

'OK, I'll leave you to it unless there's anything else?'

Keith shook his head.

'Alright to move the body now?'

'Yes, fine.'

As soon as they were alone Jack smiled at Keith. 'So you're taking Mrs Paradise's vision seriously?' Jack was the only person Keith had confided in, the only person he trusted not to ridicule him for seeking help from someone with alleged second sight.

'Experience has taught me to take her seriously,' he said, defensively.

'It's alright, I didn't mean to mock, I sort of believe in her, too.'

'OK Jack, drop it. Now, where's your father?' As he spoke they heard the sound of a car outside in the yard. John Curnow was a smaller, burlier version of his son – an open friendly face with a weathered complexion and a flat cap that seemed so permanently anchored on his head that Keith wondered whether he even took it off at bedtime. He strode forward and shook Keith's hand.

'Keith,' he said, 'how's my boy behaving?'

'Not bad,' said Keith, 'might make a policeman of him yet.'

John nodded at Jack. 'Hello son.'

'Dad.'

'Kind of you to spare the time to see us, John,' Keith said.

'I was coming over anyway,' said John Curnow. 'I was going to bury the old dog, it's what Tom would have wanted.'

What a decent man, thought Keith. 'So what can you tell me about Tom?'

'Before the accident he was a cheerful, hardworking young man with a lovely family, three happy healthy little kids and a good wife in Mandy.' John frowned. 'Well, maybe not a good wife but definitely a very good mother, she doted on those kids.'

'How do you mean "not a good wife"?' Keith asked.

'She wasn't really cut out to be a farmer's wife, not a natural like my Val. She was a city girl really, from Plymouth and found farm work hard but she made a good job of raising those children and they were lovely little kids. Sally the eldest particularly loved animals and was already helping out on the farm when it happened ...' His voice tailed away.

'And I understand from Jack that they were killed in a helicopter crash?'

'Yes,' said John, 'a terrible day. The helicopter

crashed onto the barn. There's no trace of it now, of course, but it was only a couple of fields away from our house. Val was in shock for days. The children were playing in the barn, Sally and her brother Timmy, the helicopter came down and exploded on impact.' John looked down at his feet, obviously struggling to control his emotions even after all these years.

'Did Tom and his wife see it happen?'

'His wife didn't. She was at home with the baby, but Tom did. He was on a tractor in the field above the barn, but of course he had no idea his children were in it at the time.'

'And afterwards?'

'They struggled, Tom and Mandy – they did their best but something happened to their relationship. They were both in shock, they were both in a terrible state of grieving but they couldn't seem to share that grief. Tom was a funny old boy, even then he had difficulty expressing his feelings. In the end Mandy couldn't stand it anymore – she took the baby and left.'

'Do you know where she went?' Keith asked.

'No idea.'

'And Tom accepted it, didn't try to see them?'

John shook his head. 'He thought it was best they went, get away from the place, make a fresh start for the baby away from the scene of such a tragedy.'

'Did they divorce?' Keith asked.

'No, not as far as I know. He would never talk

about her, not once she'd gone, not about her or the child. Val and I knew better than to raise the subject.'

'So,' said Keith, 'this terrible thing happened to him over thirty years ago and he waits till now to kill himself. What triggered his suicide, do you think?'

'I've been asking myself that question since I heard the news,' said John, 'and in all honesty, Keith, I haven't the least idea. Do you want to come back to the house and talk to Val? Women are always better at these things.'

Keith smiled. 'I'd like that.'

Keith Penrose always felt comfortable in the Curnows' kitchen because it reminded him so much of his own childhood home. The old Aga, the smell of baking and drying clothes. The shabby but spotless kitchen was almost a replica of the place in which he had grown up. Val Curnow greeted him warmly and he was soon seated at the table with a piping hot cup of tea and a scone.

'John reckoned you'd have a better idea as to why poor old Tom Lawson killed himself, Valerie.'

Val Curnow considered the question in silence for a moment.

'Any time in the last thirty years it wouldn't have surprised me if he had killed himself,' she said, sadly. 'Once Mandy went, his life was finished really. He went through the motions – John always thought he was a good farmer and I'm sure he's right, but his heart wasn't in it, he was just existing. The only obvious feelings he still had were for his dogs, he loved his dogs.'

'What did he farm?'

'Sheep and arable.'

'Did he make any money?'

'Enough to live on, his needs were so small. You must have seen the body?' Her eyes clouded and for a moment Keith thought she was going to cry. 'All skin and bone,' she said, 'I did my best to feed him up, but …' her voice tailed away. 'We had him up here for Sunday dinner every week, that is until the last few weeks.'

Keith frowned. 'Why did he stop coming?'

John and Val looked at each other helplessly. 'We've no idea,' said John. 'He met me in the lane a few Sundays back and said he wouldn't be coming and he hasn't been here since.'

'You didn't have an argument?' said Keith.

'Oh no, nothing like that.'

'How many weeks are we talking about?'

'Eight, nine weeks, something like that,' John said.

'And no explanation?'

'None whatsoever,' said Val, 'but he has had a visitor recently. I wondered whether that had something to do with it.'

'Who?' Keith asked.

'I don't know, I've just seen the same car there a few times and noticed because it was so unusual for Tom to have visitors other than the feed merchant.'

'What sort of car?' Keith asked.

'An old Ford Fiesta, I think,' said Val. 'I'm not very good on cars.'

'And has it been here in the last twenty-four hours?'

'I don't think so,' said Val. 'It might have been but I certainly haven't seen it.'

'Eight or nine weeks,' said Keith. 'The timing ties in with the first arson attack.'

'The boy told me about your concern that Tom might have been involved with these arson attacks,' said John. 'I have to tell you, Keith, you're barking up the wrong tree there.'

'What makes you so sure?' Keith asked.

'He wouldn't hurt a fly,' Val burst out. 'He was the gentlest, kindest man ever. The idea of him deliberately setting fire to folks' homes, particularly that one with the children – never. Besides which, he never went anywhere – Mullion occasionally, Helston very very occasionally. He had his own vegetable patch, kept a few chickens, there was always a lamb in the freezer. If I was going into town I'd always ask him if he needed a bit of shopping, usually the answer was no but occasionally he wanted something. He's barely been off the Lizard all his life. I doubt very much that he's ever been to St Ives.'

'Not sure his old Land Rover would even make it,' said John with a smile.

'Nonetheless,' Keith persisted, 'we suspect that someone with a grudge against Culdrose has been responsible for these fires and no one can be more justified than Tom Lawson in feeling vengeful so far as the Base is concerned.'

'I disagree,' said Val. 'I don't think he felt it was Culdrose's fault. They paid out good compensation, you know, which he gave to Mandy and the baby. It wasn't their fault, it was just one of those freak accidents and they lost two pilots. No one was to blame, not in Tom's eyes anyway. He was not bitter or vengeful, just ...' she searched for the right word, 'broken.'

Keith rose to his feet. 'You've been very helpful and hospitable, thanks. Now I must drag this boy of yours back to work.'

'Sorry,' said Jack, once they were back in the car. 'Wild goose chase, wasn't it? Got us absolutely nowhere.'

Keith smiled at him. 'I'm not so sure, there's a connection somehow, I just can't see it yet. I want to find Tom Lawson's wife and that baby who must be, what, over thirty now?'

'I'm on to it, sir,' Jack said.

Keith sighed. 'Let's face it, it's our best line of enquiry, or maybe I should say our only line of enquiry.'

10

The pie, thanks to Annie, was delicious, the wine also, thanks to the case her son James had given her for Christmas, and the company was unexpectedly pleasant. In her Oxford days Felicity had loved entertaining; her style had been casual, informal nursery food which Charlie and their friends seemed to love. As she brewed the coffee, a wave of nostalgia swept over her. They had talked, she and Arthur O'Sullivan, in a way she had not done for years. As the widow of a barrister, she understood his work and clearly he enjoyed that; their conversation had been wide-ranging and they now knew each other's taste in music, literature, art, newspapers, holidays and politics; they were easier, more relaxed in one another's company away from the restraints of a restaurant.

'I can't remember when I've had such a pleasant evening,' Arthur said. He'd moved from the table and was sitting in one of the two Windsor chairs which were on either side of the Aga.

'Me too,' Felicity agreed.

'It's the loss of companionship, that's what one misses most. No one to come home to, to gossip with – you turn the key in the lock, open the door and are greeted by a wall of silence.'

Felicity looked up from the coffee pot and studied him in silence for a moment. 'Yes,' she said, 'yes, you're right.' She bit her lip. 'The last time I saw Charlie, the very last time I had a conversation with him before he died, we had a row, just a silly one. If I'd known …' her voice tailed away.

Arthur leaned forward in his chair. 'You poor thing, what happened?'

'It was over nothing, trivial, the stuff that marriage is made of. I had invited some people to dinner, the Fergusons. They were friends of mine rather than Charlie's, he always found them a touch dull. He'd been working late week after week and I specifically asked him to be there that night and he said he wouldn't be. I lost my temper, he walked out and then I never saw him again, not alive anyway. Most mornings we exchanged a hug and I wished him well for his day ahead but not that morning.'

'I'm sorry,' said Arthur, 'but it's the marriage as a whole that matters, not one silly argument at the end of it.'

'I suppose so,' said Felicity. 'Did you part well with your wife? Don't tell me if you don't want to.'

'Mine was unsatisfactory, too,' Arthur said. 'Diana fought cancer for years but by the end she was riddled with it, poor dear. She had always been very close to her eldest sister, Bridget, and in the last few months Bridget moved in with us. I know it sounds childish but I felt excluded – not only did they not need me, they didn't seem to want me. On the night Diana died I was at a legal dinner. Bridget didn't even phone me to say she'd taken a turn for the worse. By the time I got home, she was already dead so I never got to say goodbye either.' The two of them stared at one another solemnly for a moment. 'My dear, do you think this friendship of ours could bring us both a little comfort, perhaps in time even a new beginning?' Arthur's gentle smile was very appealing.

'I don't know,' Felicity answered truthfully, suddenly awkward. 'Let's just see how things go, shall we Arthur?'

'Absolutely,' he said. There was a moment of tension between them.

'Tell me,' said Felicity, filling the awkward gap, 'what's happened to poor David Belcher.'

Arthur visibly relaxed back into easy territory, his work. 'An absolute mess, poor chap. He's a decent man too but losing his children like that, and then your policeman friend didn't help by arresting him when he was still in shock.'

'I suppose he was the obvious candidate,' Felicity said, quick to defend Keith. 'You read about it all the time, these terrible custody cases where the man goes off his head and kills his children rather than let his wife have them.'

'Anyone who knew David Belcher would know that was quite impossible,' said Arthur, rather pompously.

'But that's just the point, isn't it?' said Felicity. 'Keith Penrose didn't know David Belcher so he had to – how do they put it – eliminate him from his enquiries.'

'We're never going to see eye-to-eye over Chief Inspector Keith Penrose, are we?'

'No,' said Felicity with a smile, 'we're not.'

Later, as she was washing up, Felicity pondered on the obvious antagonism that lay at the heart of the relationship between Keith Penrose and Arthur O'Sullivan. She wondered whether Charlie – also a defence barrister and a good one – had been enemy number one so far as Thames Valley Police were concerned. She rather thought not, remembering the dinners he had attended with police commissioners over the years. Charlie, though, was a very different character from Arthur; everyone loved Charlie – small children, old ladies, aggressive teenagers, no nut was too hard to crack – he'd had a natural charm and a love of life that was irresistible to all. He was a tough act to follow, she thought as she scrubbed at a saucepan. Arthur had kissed her briefly on the lips when he had left – it was not an unpleasant experience but it had left her cold, no beating heart, no stirring of the loins, no rush of blood to the head. Maybe I'm just too old for all that, she thought, but still, as Arthur had said, perhaps there was room for a companion in her life.

'Keith, he's home. He's packing, he says he's leaving but he says he wants to talk to us both first. I'm sure there's something wrong, Keith, he is in a fair state.'

'I'm on my way,' said Keith, suddenly gripped with an awful weariness. He glanced at his watch. It was only just after seven o'clock. It felt as though the day had gone on for ever; a day that had begun with the difficult meeting with his Superintendent and then the viewing of Tom Lawson's body; a day in which no tangible progress had been made in any direction. Jack was still making heavy weather of tracing Mandy Lawson and her son.

His wife and son were waiting for him in the kitchen, the atmosphere around them thick as a fog. Keith drew up a chair and sat down at the kitchen table. He studied his son in silence for a moment. Visually Will favoured his mother – light brown hair, grey eyes, sharp features with a prominent chin. Physically, though, he was like his father – medium height, stocky, exuding fitness and energy in normal circumstances, but now oddly passive.

'So what's going on then, son?' Keith asked.

'I'm renting a flat in Redruth with a friend from the Army. You and Mum clearly don't want me here so I thought it was best to move on.'

'That little speech sounds more like a messed-up teenager than a man of twenty-seven.'

'Keith, please,' said Barbara, 'that's not helping.'

'I'm sorry,' said Keith, 'but I've just come from viewing the body of an old man who hung himself last night, because two of his children had died in a helicopter crash thirty years ago and his wife and baby left him. That's the stuff of real tragedy – small wonder I have little patience with teenage angst in a grown man.'

'That's always been the way, hasn't it?' said Will. 'You've always been far more wrapped up in your job than you've ever been in us.'

Suddenly all the years of criticism he'd endured from Barbara welled up inside Keith. 'Look,' he said, 'I'm here to help if that's what you want, but I'm not going to sit and listen to you moaning about my work. My work kept a roof over your head, food on the table, football boots, a new bike at Christmas. You had an idyllic childhood Will, you were loved utterly and completely by both your mother and your father. You had absolute security growing up, your friends were always welcome around here, we supported you, we were so proud of you when you got into the Army and positively dizzy with happiness when you were made a captain. I don't know what else you want from us, or expect from us, but we have nothing more to give. We love you, we're proud of you, we wish you well and we'll always be here for you but I'm not prepared to listen to any more claptrap about your neglected childhood, right?'

At which point Will Penrose burst into tears. Tissues were found; Barbara tried to hug her son but he evaded her embrace.

'I think a beer might help,' said Keith, heading towards the fridge.

'Keith, is that sensible?' said Barbara.

Keith ignored her and opened a couple of beers. 'Would you like anything?' he asked. She shook her head. Keith handed his son a bottle and sat down again, 'You've been thrown out of the Army, haven't you?' he said.

Will nodded.

'Oh, Will,' said Barbara, 'whatever did you do?'

Will took a swig of beer and addressed his father. 'I haven't been court-martialled; I was just asked to resign my commission. Nick, my friend was asked to resign as well.'

'Was it something that happened in Afghanistan?'

'Yes, we've been back in the country a couple of months now, three nearly. I needed to get my head around what happened before talking to you, so that's why I didn't contact you until a few weeks ago when the tour had finished and the regiment were home.'

'So this friend of yours, he's involved in the same problem?' Keith asked.

'Yes we've been friends for a while, since we were in Iraq. He's a major, he's a very good soldier, very brave.'

'He can't be that good a soldier if he's been asked to resign his commission,' Keith said. 'Are you going to tell us what happened?'

'We were out one day,' Will said, 'and were ambushed. Nick, my friend, had become friendly with the head man of a village not far from our base. When we got to the village we came under fire. There were Taliban everywhere, we were lucky to get out of it. It was a set-up, we lost two men, friends.'

'Oh, Will,' said Barbara, her eyes round with horror.

'Nick was furious, he thought he had developed a good relationship with the head man – trust, you know. So the following evening he took fifty of us back, he didn't get permission from higher up, he just went. We were happy to go with him, we were angry too. It was an act of revenge I suppose, certainly that's what we were told it was by our Commanding Officer afterwards.'

'So what happened?' Keith asked.

'It went terribly wrong. They were expecting us – I suppose they guessed this was how we would react. It was an absolute shambles. Of the fifty men who went out only thirty-eight came back and we lost all our kit, but worse still there was a fire.'

'What sort of fire?' Keith asked.

'There were bullets flying everywhere. There was this big house, a civilian house in the village, it was where the head man lived. It was stuffed full of women and children hiding from the fighting. I don't know what happened, it suddenly exploded into a ball of flames.' Will looked up at his father; he suddenly looked about five, vulnerable, terrified. 'It was awful, Dad. Some of them managed to escape, women running out with their babies on fire, screaming. There was screaming in the house, screaming everywhere, little children lit up like torches. I will never forget it, never get over it.'

Barbara moved round to Will's side of the table, sat beside him and took his hand in hers. This time he didn't resist her.

'And what was your pal the major doing while all this was going on?'

'Trying to keep control of his men, trying to outflank the Taliban – it was all hopeless but he saved my life, Dad.'

'How?' Keith asked.

'When the the house went up, I just froze. I stood there, I couldn't do anything. There were bullets flying all around me, I don't know why I didn't get hit and then suddenly, there was Nick. He dragged me out of it, got me into a Land Rover with a group of other men and told me to drive like hell back to barracks and I did.'

'So was that why you got drummed out of the army for deserting the fight?'

'No, no,' said Will, 'pulling the men out of the situation was the right thing to do, but it was launching the attack in the first place which was wrong. Then, of course, the loss of civilian life was terrible – from a public relations point of view too. Our Commanding Officer told us we had set back relations with the Afghans by at least a year. Of course the Taliban said it was us who set fire to the head man's house.'

'And did you?' Keith asked.

Will shrugged. 'I don't know. One of our bullets could have knocked over an oil lamp, or it could have been that there was ammunition stored in the house and the Taliban were using women and children as cover for a munitions dump. Certainly, the house went up with an enormous blast and so quickly,' he shuddered, 'but whether it was one of our bullets or one of the Taliban's, I don't know, nobody knows. Of course the story circulating is that we burnt to death a whole lot of innocent women and children.'

'So why did you do it, Will?'

'I had a lot of time for Nick, still do, and one of the lads who was killed in the first ambush was a very good mate of mine. I knew we weren't supposed to leave barracks without permission but Nick was so persuasive and we were all so angry.'

'But you knew Nick hadn't sought permission further up the line?'

'Yes, we all knew but we felt so let down. We'd been supporting this village for months, as I said we thought some trust had been built up between us and the head man and all the time we had been groomed for an ambush. It was our fight and we needed to settle it our way.'

'Instead of which a lot of innocent women and children died and even more of your men.'

'Keith, there's no need to put it like that,' Barbara said, her voice full of anguish.

'No, it's alright Mum,' said Will, 'he's right, that's how it was.'

'So what happened next?' said Keith.

'We were hauled before our Commanding Officer, we were asked to resign our commissions and we were flown home. Once we were back at the Regimental Headquarters, we were stripped of our commissions and basically turfed out on to the street. We don't even qualify for a pension, we haven't served long enough. We went to London, stayed with a friend of Nick's, went out a lot and did a lot of drinking and when the rest of the regiment came home I came down here. Nick's from Cornwall too, originally, so we came down together. I thought I could just tell you I'd left the Army and just wanted to start again with a new career and that would be the end of it, but I can't seem to settle at anything, I'm so ashamed at what happened. I can't forget the image of those people on fire, that woman carrying the bundle of flames which was her baby, I can't seem to move on – she was hugging it and it was burning her to death.'

There was a long silence.

'It seems to me,' said Keith, 'that the very worst thing you could do is to go and live with this Nick.

While you are together neither of you are ever going to be free of the memories, can never move on. I'm not saying you'll ever forget but you need to come to terms with what happened. There's stuff I've seen in my job, I will never forget, but I have to sort of file it emotionally. I can't see how you're going to be able to shake yourself free, unless you first shake yourself free of Nick.'

'I can't do that,' said Will. 'He's in a far worse state than me. It was his idea, he feels totally responsible for everything that happened and he saved my life, he definitely saved my life – I can't just walk out on him when he needs me.'

'I understand about comrades under fire. I understand that the relationship you forge with somebody when you think you're both going to die is a relationship like no other,' said Keith, 'but I'm just suggesting you spend some time apart for your sake. I'm also thinking of it from Nick's point of view. Just like he's a constant reminder for you, you're a constant reminder for him. Keep in close touch by all means, but don't live together. Stay here with us, Will, it's the best thing.'

'I can't,' said Will, 'I really can't, Dad. I need to do this, to help him through it all.'

'Have either of you thought of counselling? Wouldn't it be sensible to go to the surgery and sort some out?'

'Probably, yes, only ...'

'Only what?' Barbara asked.

'Only I'm too ashamed, Mum. Ashamed to tell anyone what's happened. That's why it's taken me so long to talk to you and Dad, I can't ever imagine feeling good about myself again, ever be able to hold my head up again.'

'I know it's an old platitude,' said Keith, 'but time is a healer, Will, this will fade. One day you will wake up and it won't be the first thing you think about.'

'I can't imagine that day ever coming,' said Will, his face haunted.

'It will and you've just got to get yourself to that place,' said Keith. 'You're going to have to be brave, far braver than you were in Afghanistan. I just wish you weren't going to live with Nick.'

Will glanced at his watch. 'I'd better get off. I arranged to meet him in the pub and I'm late. You're not going to start lecturing me about drinking, I hope,' Will said.

'I was actually,' said Keith. 'Obliterating the memories with drink isn't going to sort anything out, not in the long term.'

'Don't you think I know that Dad, I'm not a fool.' Will was on his feet now, his face red and angry. 'I'm too old for lectures, right, I'll work this out my own way. I've told you what happened, now you know.'

'Don't go like this, Will,' Barbara pleaded.

'I'm not going like anything,' said Will, 'I'm just going.'

'You'll keep in touch?' said Keith. 'You have got

my mobile number? Incidentally my superintendent was wondering whether you might consider a career in the police force.'

Will looked his father up and down. 'Dad, you just have to be joking.'

11

For Chief Inspector Keith Penrose it had been another dispiriting day. It began with the news that David Belcher had got very drunk in Helston the previous evening and had assaulted a policeman. It had taken most of the day to persuade all concerned that charges should not be pressed and he had just arranged for David's release into the care of his sister who seemed a strong-minded, intelligent woman more capable than his mother of keeping David out of trouble. There had been a short awkward interview at Helston police station during which David had sobbed and begged Keith to find the killer of his wife and children and Keith had muttered platitudes. The interview had depressed him, coming as it did on top of Will's revelations. The man was suffering so much and small wonder. Finding the person responsible for the fire wouldn't bring back his family but at least it would start the process of healing for David Belcher. While the case remained unsolved, the poor man was in a state of limbo. Horace Greenaway and his team had put in their final report on the fire at the Belchers' cottage and essentially, as anticipated, there was nothing for the police to go on. So, apart from Tom Lawson's long departed wife and son, who Jack was still having difficulty locating, and Felicity Paradise's second sight, the case was going nowhere.

Keith sat in his car outside Helston police station and looked at his watch: five-forty-five. He was not anxious to go home. Barbara seemed to be blaming him entirely for their son's predicament and probably she was right. His final words as he flung himself out of the kitchen went round and round in Keith's head, 'Dad, you just have to be joking'. Unlike a number of policemen of his age, Keith had not been in the Forces first. He had no experience of Army life but he could well imagine the brutalising effect it could have on a young man of a relatively sensitive disposition. Years ago when he was training with the Met, he remembered ending up in a bar off Piccadilly one night with a newly-discharged American soldier. They had struck up one of those chance instant friendships, that can only happen between two lonely people in a big city on a Saturday night.

The American had served in Vietnam and as he got drunker, some of the horrors and atrocities he had witnessed came pouring out. Keith had never forgotten it. It was the war on civilians that the man couldn't bear, the terrible things that had happened to women and children and Keith could quite see how Will was similarly affected by his experience in

lives you immediately assume it's all your fault and you never ever stop worrying.'

'No,' Keith agreed, grimly.

'I remember listening to a programme on the radio some years ago,' said Felicity. 'It was about motherhood. They summed up motherhood by telling the story of a ninety-eight year old woman who rang her seventy-six year old son every morning to make sure he had remembered to take his heart pills.' She was rewarded by a small smile. 'So you've a long way to go yet, Chief Inspector,' she said.

'I just don't like the sound of this Nick,' Keith said. 'While Will's still tied up with him he's never going to move on from his experiences in the Army and I can't help feeling he's a troublemaker. He was the one that appears to have got Will into this mess.'

'Why don't you ask them both out for a drink so you can have a look at him?' Felicity suggested.

'I could, I suppose, but I doubt if they'd come.'

'Well, do what you did to me this evening. Where is it he's living, Redruth?' Keith nodded. 'Say you're in Redruth and any chance of a quick pint and why not bring Nick. Come on, don't be so negative.' Felicity smiled at him.

'I'm sorry,' said Keith, 'I shouldn't have come really, I'm bad company.'

'You are,' Felicity agreed.

'So enough, let's talk about you and yours.' His expression cleared for a moment and then the frown returned. 'So did you ever go out with the odious Arthur O'Sullivan?'

'Twice,' said Felicity.

'Twice,' Keith stared at her. 'You're not …'

'Whatever you're about to ask, Chief Inspector, no I'm not, but he's good company, single and lonely like me.'

'You can't be lonely,' said Keith, 'not with your family all around you and friends and Annie and me.'

'Arthur summed it up,' said Felicity. 'It's opening the front door at the end of a long day and there being nobody there for you. He's right, it is the worst bit. I think he misses his wife very much.'

'Then he should have spent more time with her when she was alive,' said Keith. Felicity stared at him curiously. 'How do you mean?'

'Well, the poor woman was ill for years and ended up being cared for by her sister. Arthur barely saw her.'

'How do you know that?' Felicity asked.

'Common knowledge.'

'Common gossip more like.'

'Well whatever,' Keith said, 'but I've known the man for years and he's not fundamentally a nice person, so be careful. Are you seeing him again?'

'Tomorrow,' said Felicity. 'He's seeing a client in Penzance and coming by afterwards for a bit of supper. I think we're going to the Seafood Café.'

Keith looked troubled. 'As if I haven't got enough to worry about, without having to worry about you as well.'

'Keith, I think I'm just about old enough to take care of myself,' Felicity said.

'I hope so,' said Keith, once more sunk in gloom.

They talked briefly about the case but Felicity could do nothing to raise his spirits.

'Maybe he's stopped,' Felicity suggested. 'It's ten days now since the Belcher fire, maybe what happened has stopped him.'

Keith nodded. 'It bloody well should have done.'

'Isn't this the longest gap there's been between each fire, it must be? When did they start, six weeks ago?'

'Seven,' Keith corrected.

'Well there you are, maybe at least the horrors of what happened at the Belchers' home have made him stop. If we are right, if it was genuinely a case of mistaken identity and the arsonist got the wrong cottage, he must be in pieces. Look, I'm probably being a bit naive here, but have you considered how the arsonist knows there's a Culdrose connection in each case? You're a policeman and you didn't know that Philip Ferguson had been a helicopter pilot before he became a travel writer. Maybe the person you're looking for is actually someone on the base who has access to personnel records.'

'Possibly,' said Keith, 'but that wouldn't stack up with the St Ives cottage. The Turners had no connection with the Base at all other than the fact that their son, Gary, is there. Their details wouldn't have appeared in the personnel records. I'd have thought it is more likely that it is somebody local who knows the background of the families concerned.'

'That's creepy,' said Felicity. 'Someone right here in our midst.'

'Maybe,' Keith said.

'Dad!'

So absorbed had they been in their conversation that they had not seen two young men enter the bar. One had headed straight for the bar and was now ordering drinks, the other, somewhat hesitantly, had approached the table where Felicity and Keith sat. Keith jumped to his feet.

'Will!' he said, putting his arm on his shoulder. He hesitated and looked at Felicity. 'Felicity, this is my son, Will. Will, this is Felicity Paradise.' They shook hands – a nice-looking boy, Felicity thought, but she could see a shadow hanging over him; he was worried, upset, preoccupied, miserable. 'What are you doing here?' Keith asked.

'Oh, Nick and I are having a drink. That's Nick over there.' On hearing his name the man standing by the bar turned and raised an arm in greeting but made no attempt to come over to the table. 'He's not very sociable at the moment,' Will said. 'Sorry.'

'I understand,' said Keith. 'So you don't want to join us, or could I come and meet Nick?'

'I don't think so,' said Will.

'Have you, have you settled in alright?'

'I'm fine Dad, no worries. See you soon.' He

nodded at Felicity and went back up to the bar.

'So that's the infamous Nick,' said Felicity in a stage whisper. 'Given that he was largely responsible for your son being drummed out of the Army you'd think he'd at least have come and said hello.'

'That's probably why he hasn't come to say hello,' said Keith. Felicity studied the boys over Keith's shoulder.

'Don't stare,' said Keith.

'I'm not,' said Felicity, 'I'm observing them, they've got their backs to me anyway. Will seems to be doing all the talking. He looks like he's trying to reassure Nick – oops, they're on the move.' Nick drowned his pint and without a glance in their direction headed for the door, Will in his wake.

'That was pretty odd,' said Felicity, as the door closed behind them. She glanced at Keith, who was looking decidedly dejected. 'At least he came over to talk to you, he was quite friendly,' she said, putting a hand on his arm.

'I just don't like it,' said Keith. 'I don't like the hold that Nick seems to have over Will.'

'Well, from what you've said they've been in the Army together for some while and I'm sure when you're in a situation where you're under fire with somebody, you must get terribly close.' She tried to make light of it. 'Look at us, we've had a near-death experience together and been good pals ever since.'

Keith rewarded her with a smile. 'That's very true, Mrs Paradise, and I can only apologise again for boring you silly with my domestic problems.'

'I've bored you silly often enough with mine,' said Felicity. 'Seriously though, Keith, think about it – two young men in constant danger together day after day and then they make this silly decision to go and teach the Taliban a lesson. They end up losing their men, seeing appalling atrocities and then being forced out of the Army in disgrace, it's bound to make them close …' her voice tailed away. 'I didn't like the look of Nick though, did you?'

'It's hard to say,' said Keith. 'It was difficult to get a proper look at him without appearing rude.'

'There was a cloud hanging over both of them, not surprising, of course. I could see your Will was a nice chap, but as for Nick, you know how Buddhists talk about auras around people? Well, his aura was all red and angry and full of hate.'

'Those are strong words,' Keith said.

'I know. I'm not trying to alarm you, I'm just saying there is something very wrong with that young man.'

12

Jack Curnow was already waiting for his boss when Keith arrived at the office the following morning.

'I sense a breakthrough,' said Keith, without a great deal of conviction.

'I'm afraid that's going a bit far,' said Jack, 'but I have made some progress with the Lawsons.'

'Right,' said Keith, 'I'm all ears.'

Jack consulted his notebook.

'As you know, Tom Lawson's wife was called Mandy. After the fire which killed their elder children, Sally and Tim, Mandy took the baby and moved back to Plymouth because her sister Amy lived there. Amy's husband was in the Navy. For the first few years the sisters were virtually neighbours. Amy looked after the baby so that Mandy could work part time and she got a job in W.H. Smith – apparently she had worked for the company before when she had just left school.'

'I suppose that's what your parents were meaning the other day,' said Keith, 'a girl straight out of W.H.

Smith's in Plymouth hasn't got much experience of farming on the Lizard.'

'Exactly,' said Jack. 'Unfortunately Mandy has died. She died ten years ago of breast cancer. I managed to get hold of Amy who now lives near Reading, at Thatcham, since her husband retired. Apparently Mandy made very little effort to fight the cancer – she'd never got over the death of her first two children, and just faded away.'

'And the baby?' Keith asked.

'The baby was twenty-two by the time his mother died. He sold up the little flat in which they'd lived and, according to his aunt, has never had a home since. She's barely seen him since his mother's funeral. He joined the Army and she believes the Army has become his family.'

'So have you managed to trace him, where is he?'

'Well, that's where it all gets a bit difficult.'

'Why's that?' Keith asked, a prickle of apprehension appearing from nowhere.

'Mandy's youngest son is called Nicholas. I contacted the army and after some fairly torturous twists and turns established that he was dishonourably discharged three months ago and they have no idea of his whereabouts.'

Keith let the information sink in for a moment. 'So you think Nicholas Lawson could be Will's friend Nick?'

'I don't think so, I know.'

'How?' Keith asked.

'There didn't seem much point in pussyfooting about. I have Will's mobile number, I simply rang him and asked him if his friend Nick's surname was Lawson.'

'When was this?' Keith asked.

'Last night.'

'What did he say?' Keith asked.

'He was very defensive to start with, wanted to know why I needed to know so I simply told him that I was trying to trace the whereabouts of Tom Lawson's next-of-kin because sadly he had committed suicide. Will said that Nick already knew about his father's death and wanted to be left alone so I just played the community cop and said he needed to arrange a funeral and that sort of thing and if he wanted any help or advice to organise things to give me a ring. He hasn't of course.'

'So what you're really saying,' said Keith, pushing back the chair and running a hand through his hair, 'is that my son's best mate is the number one suspect for these arson attacks?'

'It fits,' said Jack. 'They were asked to resign their commissions about a month before the arson attacks began. Did you realise Will had been discharged from the Army?'

Keith nodded. 'Yes, yes he told Barbara and I the other night. They went to London first, apparently, and laid low there until the rest of their regiment came home from Afghanistan. I think his initial intention had been not to tell Barbara and me what had happened.'

'And what did happen, if you don't mind me asking sir?'

With a heavy heart Keith told Jack of Will's experiences in Afghanistan.

'Blimey,' said Jack, 'fire again.'

'Yes,' said Keith, 'I was thinking the same thing. So what we've got here, Jack, is a young man, deeply disturbed. His family were split up when he was still a baby because his older brother and sister were killed by a Culdrose helicopter – which effectively meant they burnt to death. His father then became a recluse. Is there any evidence Nick had much contact with his father?'

'According to Amy none at all, but I think they may have met recently.'

'The car your parents were talking about?'

'Yes, I'm obviously only guessing but it occurs to me that Nick may have made some effort to contact his father on his return to Cornwall.'

Keith nodded. 'So back in Cornwall he starts setting fire to cottages associated with Culdrose, but presumably in the case of the Belchers', he got the wrong cottage …'

'Which given his background must have been terrible for him,' Jack concluded.

'He must have been half off his head having killed those children and it could be why the old man killed himself, if he knew what his son was up to.'

'I still don't understand how he knew which

cottages to target?' said Jack.

'Hearsay, pub talk, he's a big pub man apparently.'

The two men were silent for a moment. Keith broke the silence. 'The question we have to ask ourselves now, Jack, is whether Will is involved with this because if so, I must come off the case immediately.'

'I don't think so,' said Jack loyally.

'The two of them are thick as thieves, Jack. How could Will not know what was going on? I saw them last night in the Sloop, I was having a drink with Mrs Paradise and they came in.'

'What's he like, this Nick?'

'Hard to tell, he wouldn't come and say hello. Will came over and was quite pleasant and then they left before they'd hardly arrived.'

'If he is the arsonist, he's hardly likely to have been comfortable in the same pub as you, with all due respect,' said Jack.

'No, that's true,' said Keith. 'Look Jack, I'm going to have to see the Super before we take this any further.'

'Don't be too long. I think we ought to pick him up, we don't want him running off.'

'He and Will have just acquired a flat in Redruth, I can't imagine he's planning to do a runner.'

'Unless my call to Will has made him think we're on to him.'

Keith nodded. 'I'll try and see the boss right now.'

Keith stood up and hurried towards the door. He looked exhausted and Jack hated being responsible for the news he'd had to impart. He did not know Will Penrose that well, but he'd known him a long time and his instincts told him that Will was not involved. But who knows, Army life could have changed him, must have changed him. Given what he had been through, anything was possible. Keith was almost out of the door when a thought occurred to Jack.

'Sir?'

'What?' Keith asked, his face grey and strained.

'There's still Mrs Paradise's theory which might help us. It's only two weeks since the Belcher fire; if he did catch his gloves alight, there will still be scars.'

'And according to Mrs Paradise, he was alone, wasn't he?' Keith said, clearly grateful for the spark of hope.

Jack nodded. 'So she says.'

'Certainly Mrs Paradise was quite clear that it was a man on his own, so maybe …' Keith began.

'So maybe Will isn't involved,' Jack finished for him.

Superintendent George Staple was known to be tough but fair, a man of few words but what he did have to say was always relevant, appropriate and normally made a great deal of sense. What he was not known for was his sensitivity. The distressed state of his Chief Inspector was all too evident, and as a father himself, George Staple was not surprised. It was every parent's nightmare, every policeman's hell on earth – your own child in the frame, a suspect, possibly even a killer – he shuddered inwardly as he faced Keith across the width of his desk, but could provide no words of comfort.

'You of course were completely right to come and see me, Keith,' he said. 'I'll arrange for someone to pick up the young men and we'll have them taken to Helston police station. You just stay out of it informally until we've established your boy's involvement. If he's in the clear then the case is still yours. Is that fair?'

'Very fair, sir, thank you.'

'I'll keep you in the picture.' George stood up, interview clearly over. Keith headed towards the door. 'Oh, Keith, what is the name of that sergeant of yours?'

'Jack Curnow.'

'Jack can tag along with the arresting officers, if you like. He can provide some continuity and keep you up to speed with developments as well.'

'Thank you very much sir,' said Keith again.

'Good luck,' George said under his breath as the door closed.

For an hour and a half Keith sat miserably at his desk quite incapable of any thought or action while he waited for news. What was taking them so long? He couldn't believe that Jack would not at least let him know what had happened to Will. Finally there was a telephone call.

'They've gone,' said Jack without preamble.

'How do you mean, gone?' Keith asked.

'We approached the house very discreetly and there was no back entrance,' Jack said, 'it's one of those terraces where the houses back to back with another terrace and only have front gardens. They couldn't have seen us coming and if they had, there was no escape. In my view, they've been gone for some while.'

'How do you know they haven't just gone out?'

'Because their clothes are missing and their personal possessions,' Jack replied. 'There was also a note for the landlord giving a week's notice and leaving him the cash.'

'Well at least they didn't do a moonlight flit,' Keith said.

'No,' Jack agreed. 'They'd left the place tidy, clean, washing-up done, bed stripped, Army discipline, I suppose. You couldn't fault them, sir, it's just that they're not here. I shouldn't have made that call to Will. It wasn't even because I truly suspected that his friend was Nick Lawson – it was more to eliminate him from enquiries.'

'The fact that they've gone,' Keith interrupted, miserably, 'suggests they are guilty, doesn't it? They've only just moved into that flat – why leave it unless they've something to hide, unless they're on the run?'

'Let's not jump to any conclusions, until we

know the facts,' said Jack. 'They can't have got far, we'll pick them up.'

'I hope you're right,' said Keith.

'What are you going to do, sir, until there's some news?' Jack's voice was full of sympathy.

'What I've been putting off for the last hour,' said Keith. 'I'm going to have to tell Barbara.'

Barbara Penrose finished work at three o'clock on Wednesdays and Keith was waiting for her at home when she let herself through the front door.

'Keith,' she said, startled. 'What on earth are you doing here?' Then she took one look at his face. 'Oh, my God,' she said, 'what's wrong, what's happened, is it Carly?'

Keith stood up. 'No, no,' he said, 'nothing's happened, nobody's hurt or ill, promise. Would you like a cup of tea?'

'Keith, for God's sake just tell me what's going on.'

'It's Will,' said Keith, 'he could be in trouble.'

Barbara's eyes widened. 'With the law?'

Keith nodded. 'That friend of his, Nick, he could be our local arsonist.'

'But not Will,' said Barbara, 'Will wouldn't … oh my God, those children.' She sat down at the kitchen table and put her head in her hands. For a moment neither of them spoke. 'What makes you think they're involved?' Barbara asked. Keith told her the whole story. 'So you think their experiences in

Afghanistan triggered Nick's need to take revenge on Culdrose?'

'That's the theory we're working on,' said Keith.

'And you think Will's helping him?' Barbara's face had suddenly become very pinched.

'Barbara, I just don't know,' said Keith, 'they've become very close since their discharge from the Army, that cannot be disputed, but I'm sure if he is guilty Nick kept those attacks to himself. It's just that ...'

'It's just that what?' Barbara asked.

'Jack Curnow rang Will to find out the surname of his friend. He used the excuse that he was trying to locate Tom Lawson's next-of-kin. Will told him it was, he didn't hold back, but now the pair of them have done a bunk which could suggest they're in it together.'

'Oh my God,' said Barbara, 'does the Super know?'

Keith nodded. 'I'm off the case until we've established Will's innocence.'

'The press,' said Barbara. 'It'll be all over the press, all our friends will know, people at work.'

The well of anger and misery that had been building in Keith all day exploded at her words. 'For Christ's sake,' he said, 'what the hell does it matter what our friends and your work colleagues think, what does it matter what anybody thinks? Arson is a serious criminal offence and in this case linked to the deaths of four people – three of them tiny children. We are talking a very long custodial sentence – Will's life will be over, finished, if he's involved in this. By the time he emerges from prison he'll be in his fifties, brutalised by the system without the chance of a wife or children and with us too bloody old, if we're still alive, to be any use to him at all – and you're worried about what your friends will think?'

'It's your fault,' Barbara said. 'If you'd been …'

'I wondered how long it would take us to get round to that again,' said Keith. 'I'm not saying I'm an ideal husband or father, Barbara, but I'm hardly a monster. During his formative years at least I showed Will what the work ethic was and my job of work is trying to uphold the law. I wasn't torturing small animals in a laboratory or selling crack on a street corner; I wasn't a used-car salesman selling deathtraps for exorbitant prices or some slimy politician no longer knowing the difference between truth and a lie. I did my best.'

'Which wasn't good enough,' Barbara said, her voice as hard as nails. 'It was so obvious Carly was your favourite because she was a cross-country runner like you, because she was good at exams like you, because she idolised her Daddy and pandered to your ego.'

'I'm sorry,' said Keith. 'I simply can't listen to any more of this.' And with that, he left the kitchen, closing the front door quietly behind him and getting into his car to drive, he knew not where.

13

He might be extremely small but he had taken command of his new home totally and seamlessly. He had also seemed to have taken it for granted that Felicity's role was that of an adoring slave and supervisor of his fan club, for Harvey enslaved everyone he met. Annie kept making pathetic excuses to pop round, clearly to see the puppy. Mel had been late for work twice as Harvey had come with Felicity to babysit and Mel had found it quite impossible to tear herself away from this new member of the family. This had particularly amused Felicity since Mel had been dead against her mother's having a dog, particularly a Jack Russell.

'There're horror stories all the time about Jack Russells eating babies,' Mel had grumbled. 'Anyway you don't need a dog, it'd tie you down.'

'I want to be tied down,' said Felicity, 'and the puppy will be fine with Minty, they'll grow up together.' Further persuasion had been quite unnecessary since Harvey had asserted his charm. Mel and Martin were completely under his spell.

Felicity was sitting on the floor of her kitchen trying to extract a sock from Harvey's mouth. It had fallen out of the laundry basket earlier and he had been carrying it around the house like a trophy.

'Harvey, I really need this back before you tear it to shreds,' Felicity said, but the needle-sharp teeth were firmly embedded – it was not going to be an easy job. Her mobile rang and in the time it took her to extract it from the pocket of her trousers, Harvey had disappeared with the sock under an armchair where he was growling at it triumphantly.

'I wondered if you were free for a drink tonight?' It was Keith Penrose and he sounded weird.

'No, I'm not, I'm so sorry,' said Felicity, 'I'm having dinner with Arthur.'

'Never mind then,' said Keith, clearly about to end the conversation.

'Keith, what's wrong?'

'Nothing,' said Keith. 'Well, everything really but I can't go into it now. We'll catch up soon, take care.' And he was gone.

Felicity stared at the mobile, tempted to ring him back, and then thought better of it. He was probably still at work and in a hurry, though instinct told her it was more than that. She glanced at her watch; it was ten past six. She turned on the television – while she prepared supper for Harvey, she might as well catch any local news, in case this was what was upsetting Keith. There was no news of any consequence.

She was due to meet Arthur at seven-fifteen at the Seafood Café and she didn't really want to go, she realised, as she rummaged around for a clean shirt. It was not a good sign. She would far rather have had a drink with Keith or, she had to admit, stayed at home with her new baby who was still strutting round the house, sock in mouth, looking really pleased with himself. She enjoyed Arthur's company but not enough, she thought. She dragged a brush through her hair and considered her reflection in the mirror – some lipstick, some eyeliner – that would have to do. It was not that she didn't like him; she did, but she had wondered more than once whether it would have been better if he had not been a lawyer. He liked to talk about his work and she was interested, but every time they discussed it, it was like an echo from the past, like the many times she and Charlie had sat together talking in their basement kitchen over a glass of wine while Charlie tried to unravel his thoughts on a particularly tricky case. The trouble was this pleasant, good-looking man was not Charlie and never would come close in her affections, whatever he said or did.

'I think you're going to be the only man in my life, Harvey,' Felicity called up the stairs from the bathroom.

Three hours later, Felicity was back in the cottage and preparing to take Harvey for his late night constitutional. It had been a pleasant enough evening. Arthur had been amusing and attentive and clearly had been angling for an invitation back to Jericho Cottage which had not been forthcoming. Harvey had provided the excuse. She had already established that Arthur was not an animal lover so the mention of puppy pees and poos all over her kitchen had done the trick. Hovering at the back of her mind throughout the evening had been the brief telephone call from Keith. While there had been nothing on the evening news to suggest there was any development in the arson cases, or anything else come to that, she could sense from his voice that something was horribly wrong.

She took Harvey down to the harbour. He was too small to be let off the lead. He still needed his final jabs before he could walk on pavements, but she carried him down on to the harbour sand, newly washed by the tide. They wandered about together and Harvey did some growling at one or two seagulls which were about three times his size and were singularly unimpressed. Felicity glanced up at the church clock, it was only just after ten and yet the town was deserted tonight despite the fact that it was a beautiful evening. There appeared to be nobody on the Wharf and just a few hardened smokers sitting outside the Sloop.

Suddenly she heard raised voices. There were two men standing at the top of the slipway, clearly arguing. For a moment she hesitated. They were probably drunk so perhaps she should find another way off the beach, but they were so intent on their argument that they didn't even notice Felicity and Harvey as they walked quietly up the other side of the slipway. The larger of the two men was punching his companion in the shoulder, obviously trying to provoke a fight. Felicity hurried by them, head down, anxious not to attract attention but still she caught snatches of conversation as she passed them.

'Why don't you just tell me?' the smaller man was saying.

'Why don't you just mind your own sodding business?'

'It is my business.'

'No it's not.'

Felicity glanced up. Just for a second, the face of the smaller man was illuminated by the street lamp. It was Will Penrose and he looked scared. As soon as she and Harvey were home, Felicity called Keith but his mobile was switched off.

Will Penrose woke the following morning with a hangover from hell, accompanied by a splitting head. He was lying on the sofa in the rather scruffy sitting room of a flat at the top end of Bedford Road. It had been loaned to them by the older sister of a school friend of Will's; they had it for two weeks until the sister returned. Will tried to get his brain in gear but it was still muddled from the night before. He swung his legs over the side of the sofa and sat up. He was stiff, exhausted and scared. Fuelled by drink, Nick had more or less admitted to the arson attacks the previous evening, but if he was responsible for them, then he was also responsible for the deaths of the Belcher woman and children in the Halsetown cottage – history repeating itself. A knot formed in Will's stomach and for a moment he wondered if he was going to be sick; the feeling passed. Will knew he should contact his father, not run away as they had done following Jack Curnow's call, but something had stopped him; pride, maybe. He tried to imagine how his father would react if he unloaded his suspicions. Would he crow, would he say 'I told you so'? No, in fairness, thought Will, that was not his style at all. He stood up gingerly, his head swimming. If he took a shower and had a coffee, hopefully he would be able to decide what to do next.

It was after ten before Felicity made contact with Keith. 'You've had your mobile switched off,' she said, accusingly.

'Yes, I have,' said Keith, offering no explanation.

'Are you going to tell me what's wrong?' Felicity persisted.

'No,' Keith answered, 'not at the moment, I don't think so.'

'Can I do anything to help?'

'No, thank you,' Keith replied. 'Did you have a good evening?'

'It was alright,' said Felicity, 'he's a bit of an old

bore, not nearly as much fun as Charlie.' There was an awkward pause. 'Keith, the reason I was ringing is that I saw Will last night.'

It was as if she had lit a fuse. 'Will, my Will?'

'Yes.'

'Where did you see him?'

'In St Ives.'

'What was he doing, who was he with, what time was this?'

'Hang on, hang on, this isn't an interrogation! I'll tell you; just give me a moment to get the words out.'

'Sorry,' he said, 'only we're – I'm – trying to find him.'

'Certainly last night at about ten o'clock he was in St Ives,' said Felicity. 'He was with his friend, Nick, I assume – it looked like him, only I didn't get a chance to see his face, and they were arguing.'

'Where was this?' Keith asked.

'They were at the top of the slipway just by the Sloop. I think they'd been drinking, they were certainly very loud.'

'Arguing – did you hear what they said?'

'Not really, no.'

'And did you see which way they went?'

'No, I didn't,' said Felicity, 'to be honest I was trying not to get involved. I have taken delivery of my puppy now and we'd just gone for a walk on the beach. Actually, so far as I was concerned, they were just a couple of drunks who I was anxious to avoid. It was only as I was walking past them I saw that one of them was Will.'

'I wonder if they're staying in the town?' Keith said. 'Thanks, that's really helpful. I wish I'd known about it last night.'

'I did try to ring you,' said Felicity, 'but your phone was off, if you remember.'

'Sorry, yes thanks,' said Keith, distractedly, 'I'll be in touch.' The line went dead. Whatever was wrong with Keith, he was clearly not going to share it with her. Felicity felt sadly hurt – didn't he trust her? Obviously, whatever his problems, they revolved around Will and from what he had said, a slip of the tongue – 'we' instead of 'I', it sounded as though Will could be in trouble with the police. Small wonder Keith didn't want to discuss the matter, Felicity thought – poor man.

Taking her coffee, Felicity went out onto the balcony. It was a beautiful early summer morning. She could see that down by the harbour there was quite a breeze, the sea whipped up so that it was boiling into the harbour, but here on her balcony, sheltered from the wind, it could have been mid-summer. She sat down on a chair and sipped her coffee. It was her day off – no school, no Minty, she could please herself. She was completely free apart from the tyranny being exercised by one small dog. She glanced into the kitchen where the tyrant in question was deeply unconscious in his basket by the Aga. She would finish her coffee and then take him for a carry around the Island and a romp on the beach.

'Jack.'

'Good morning sir, no progress I'm afraid.'

'There's been a sighting,' said Keith. 'Mrs Paradise saw them last night outside the Sloop in St Ives.'

'What time was this?'

'About ten,' said Keith. 'Of course they could have gone anywhere for the night but my feeling is they're probably still there.'

'Well, that's a relief,' Jack said. 'We were starting to think they'd probably gone up-country.'

'Me too,' said Keith.

'I'll get some officers over there right away,' said Jack. 'If they're still in town we'll find them.'

'You'll go too?' Keith said.

'Yes, of course,' said Jack.

'Then I'll see you there.'

'Sir, I don't think you should come ...'

'I won't interfere Jack, but I've got to be there, you must see that.'

After a shower, Will had tried to ring his father but his mobile was engaged. He made himself a cup of coffee and stood in the bleak little kitchen trying to decide what he should be doing. Since their return to the UK, Nick's behaviour had become more and more erratic. He was aggressive, secretive, yet clearly

170

very dependent on Will. Was it possible he was responsible for the arson attacks and, if so, why? After the horrors of Afghanistan, Will thought, Nick should have had more than enough of fire and its consequences.

There was a sound of movement overhead and footsteps on the stairs. Will felt an overwhelming sense of dread. I need to get out of this situation, he thought, but how? He owed this man his life. But for Nick there was no question that he would be dead. To walk away now would be just as much an act of supreme cowardice as the one in Afghanistan which had paralysed him with fear.

The kitchen door swung open and Nick walked in. Much to Will's surprise he was fully dressed including his jacket.

'Considering last night's skinful you're very together this morning. Are you going somewhere?'

'Is there any coffee?' Nick asked.

'I found the dregs of a jar,' said Will. 'It's fairly repellent but I think there is definitely the makings of a caffeine shot there. Would you like one?'

Nick nodded. 'I think we should go back up-country, Will, there's nothing down here for us, particularly now my old man's dead. Ironic really, I finally catch up with him and then he goes and tops himself.' It was the first time Nick had been prepared to talk about his father.

'Why did he do it, Nick?' Will handed him a mug of coffee.

'Don't know, don't care.'

'That can't be right,' said Will. 'I thought you two were starting to get to know one another, I thought things were going well.'

'Just shut up will you, Will, you don't know what the hell you're talking about.'

'OK, OK,' said Will. 'But I'm not sure I want to go back up-country. I'm lucky, I know that, but I still have my family here.'

'I thought you couldn't stand your family – mother nagging all the time, father a sodding cop – I thought you couldn't wait to put some distance between you and them.'

'It is difficult being at home after all these years of Army life, but I'm not saying I never want to see them again.'

'You're lucky to have the choice,' said Nick.

'I appreciate that,' said Will. 'I still don't see what the rush was to get out of the Redruth flat, you're far more likely to get work over there than here. It was a good flat, comfortable.'

'As I said, the landlord changed his mind. He wanted the flat for a friend of his.'

'I don't understand it,' Will began, 'I saw him the day before and he was fine.'

'Just drop it Will, will you.' Nick's green eyes were glinting dangerously, his temper very close to the surface these days.

'Whatever,' said Will. 'Anyway maybe it's time we split – you go back up-country and I'll see how I get on with a job down here.'

'So, abandoning me, are you, to go back to Mummy after all I've done for you?'

'No, it's just that...' Will began when the doorbell rang. 'I wonder who that is?' he said, making for the door of the kitchen.

'Don't answer it,' said Nick. 'Come and stand in the hall away from the windows until they've gone.'

'What!' said Will, heading towards the door. 'I'll just go and see who it is.'

'You won't,' said Nick.

Will turned to his friend in surprise to find that he was holding a gun and that the pistol was aimed right at his chest.

'Stop fooling around, Nick,' he said nervously. 'And where the bloody hell did you get that gun anyway?'

'I'm not fooling around,' said Nick, 'it's the police at the door, they're doing a house-to-house. I've been watching them from the upstairs window. Don't you dare make a sound until they've given up and gone away. They won't try to break in if they don't know we're here.'

'Why would it matter if they did know we were here?' Will asked, his eyes still on the gun.

'You really don't understand, do you?' said Nick.

'When you were drunk last night, you started talking about the arson attacks,' Will began.

'Shut it, mummy's boy,' Nick hissed. 'Now just stand absolutely still and don't make a sound.'

The doorbell rang again. Will hesitated.

'I mean it, Will,' said Nick. 'I'll use it if I have to.' The two men fell silent for a moment, Will still eyeing the gun. He had no doubts in his mind that Nick meant exactly what he said. There was a wild irrationality about him, that and the fact that he had been trained to be a killer, and was brutalised by his experiences in Afghanistan. It felt as if he was capable of anything, including killing his friend if he stood in his way.

'They've gone,' Nick said after a moment or two. 'Now, get your stuff, we're off.' He made no attempt to lower the gun.

'You go,' said Will. 'I'm not coming with you. I think I'll go back and make my peace with my parents.'

'You're coming with me. You're my insurance policy out of here,' said Nick. 'Now get your stuff.'

Moments later the two men left the house in Bedford Road. The car was in Porthgwidden car park.

'We'll go via the Island,' said Nick. 'As the police are doing a house-to-house, it'll probably be the best route to Porthgwidden – I doubt they'll be looking for us in the Tate.' He placed the pistol in the pocket of his jacket. 'It's here Will, and I will use it if I have to.'

'I still don't understand why you need me in this,' said Will.

'You can be a thick bastard sometimes,' said Nick. 'Let me explain it to you in simple terms, you're in a hostage situation and you are it – the hostage.

Now for Christ's sake, get a move on, I don't want them sealing off the town before we're out of here.'

Keith Penrose had kept in radio contact as he drove to St Ives. The house-to-house had produced nothing so far but the landlord of the Sloop had confirmed that two men, fitting Will's and Nick's descriptions, had argued in the pub the night before and had been sufficiently drunk and noisy that he had asked them to leave. The timing fitted in exactly with Felicity Paradise's sighting. They had definitely been in town last night; the question was where were they now? Half way along the A30, Keith's mobile had bleeped and informed him there was a missed call. The number was a landline in the Penzance/St Ives area – 01736. He tried the number but there was no reply. Could it have been Will trying to make contact? Probably not, and yet, somewhere deep inside him, Keith felt his boy was in trouble, that his life was on the line. It was not an unfamiliar feeling. During Will's tours of Iraq and Afghanistan, thoughts of his son would pop into his mind at unexpected moments and every time it happened he assumed the boy was in danger. He would spend the next twenty-four hours fretting, expecting news of the worst kind, which mercifully never happened. He felt the same now.

The radio crackled into life, it was Jack's voice. 'Sir, there's been a sighting. They're moving along Porthmeor beach towards the Island, we're closing in now.'

'I'm already in town,' said Keith, 'I'll be with you in seconds.'

Felicity and Harvey were sitting on a bench on the Island, overlooking Porthmeor beach; they were watching the surfers. It was a wonderful day for surfing, set after set coming in big and clean.

'Maybe I should take up body-boarding,' Felicity said conversationally to Harvey, who gave her what she thought was rather a pitying look. 'OK, I'm no spring chicken, but it's never too late to learn something new.' Harvey dropped his head with a theatrical sigh then suddenly, his body stiffened. He was looking beyond her to two men walking towards her. One of them she recognised immediately as Will Penrose. She stood up and smiled a greeting.

'Hello Will, I don't know if you remember me, I'm a friend of your father's.'

The boy returned her smile but with a nervous one. 'Oh yes,' he began.

Things happened very quickly. Three policemen appeared at the top of the steps from the beach, one of whom Felicity recognised as Jack Curnow, Keith's sergeant.

'Nicholas Lawson, William Penrose, stop right there please,' he shouted, his voice carrying on the wind.

'No,' shouted Nick, 'you stop right there, I have a gun and I'm not afraid to use it.'

And indeed he had. Felicity stared at the gun

which had suddenly appeared and then at Will who looked as frightened as she did. Jack stopped, a few yards from them now.

'Just hand the gun over sir, we don't want anybody getting hurt.'

'I don't care a damn if anyone gets hurt, now back off.' He grabbed Felicity by the arm, the muzzle of the gun just a few inches from her head. 'I'll use it,' he said, 'and I'll use it on the lady first. Stay right where you are and don't try any heroics. We're going over the island.'

'Let her go, Nick,' Will said desperately, 'don't involve her! You don't need two hostages, you've got me.'

'Shut up!'

Harvey, who was now on the ground, was growling and bravely tugging at Nick's trouser leg. Nick shook his leg free and gave Harvey a vicious kick so that the puppy sailed into the air yelping piteously, his little body falling over the cliff to the beach below. Felicity's screams were swallowed up by the wind.

14

Keith abandoned his car at the entrance to Porthgwidden car park, threw his car keys at the parking attendant and headed across the car park towards the Island. He was on the edge of the grass when he saw them, Felicity and Will, scrambling up the hill towards the Chapel with Nick Lawson behind them, a gun trained on them. He could see the gun clearly, the sunlight catching the metal. He ducked down behind a parked car, terror gripping him. Two of the people he cared most about in the world threatened by a madman with a gun, and a madman was what Nicholas Lawson was, he was sure of it. The previous evening he had managed to contact Nick's and Will's former Commanding Officer who had confirmed that Nicholas Lawson was out of control and capable of anything, which was why the Army was no place for him any longer. He more or less admitted to Keith that Will had been a scapegoat and was not directly to blame for the raid. However, the fact that he had been so easily led meant he too was no longer suitable officer material. From his position behind the parked car Keith could see his sergeant accompanied by two other officers. Jack was on the radio; in his hurry Keith had left his in the car. Jack would be calling for an armed response team but that would take time, it would be an hour or an hour and a half before they reached St Ives. It would all be over by then, one way or another.

The gunman and his two hostages had reached the Chapel now. Nick was gazing around him, his gun still trained on Will. Felicity, it appeared, had collapsed on the ground. The men, Army-trained, would have had no trouble at all climbing the hill at speed – a different matter for Felicity. What now? Keith tried to put himself in Nick Lawson's position. It wouldn't take him very long to work out that provided he moved quickly, the chances of encountering a policeman with a gun here in St Ives were negligible. Early in the season though it was, the town was full of visitors and he'd also assume, rightly, that the police wouldn't risk a shoot-out where innocent people could get hurt. Mercifully at the moment, it was early enough for the Island to be almost deserted. There were one or two people in the car park and a couple walking a dog round the Island path – otherwise, there was no one.

Why had he Felicity with him as well as Will, why two hostages? Keith frowned. Trust her to be in the very thick of it, he thought. What would I do, what would I do now, he thought, if I were Nick. He glanced again at Jack. It was tempting to join his colleagues, but if Nick chose to come down to Porthgwidden car park Keith was in a perfect position. If he made his whereabouts known to Jack then he would make them known to Nick as well. He prayed Jack wouldn't try to rush him but there seemed no chance of that, he was staying well back. He had the good sense and training to recognise an extremely dangerous situation when he saw one. Somehow Keith had to stop them getting to a car. A car doubles the danger for hostages – not only was there a gun but also the risk of a car crash. They could road-block the A30, of course, make it almost impossible to get out of the Duchy, but catching Army-trained Nick Lawson after he got out of St Ives was not going to be that easy, Keith sensed. What to do, how to stop him?

Keith was well aware of the vulnerability of his position and the chances of being spotted. Nick Lawson at the top of the hill could easily see him crouching behind the car if he chose to look, but Keith was banking on the fact that he would not. His main concerns would be Jack and his party, the possibility of other officers appearing down in the car park – which Keith imagined was his destination – and the unpredictable behaviour of his hostages. It was inevitable that Will would have a go at some stage – Keith just hoped he would get his moment right – and as for Felicity, she was a loose cannon, she could do anything. He felt sick with nerves.

As predicted Nick Lawson was not going to hang

about by the Chapel, probably assuming that Jack would have other men and resources on their way. He began moving down the grassy slope towards the car park, Felicity and Will in front of him once more. Lawson was shouting at them but Keith could not catch his words for the wind was blowing them out to sea. They were going purposely down the hill; the car had to be in the middle of the car park somewhere. Keith began very, very slowly edging his way behind the parked cars heading towards the spot where the party would reach the edge of the car park. He was aware that any movement he made could easily catch Nick's eye, aware again that this was a man Army-trained to have eyes in the back of his head. They must not reach the car. As Keith drew nearer to them, he saw that Will was holding Felicity's hand, helping her down the slope. Lawson was still hurling abuse, presumably urging them to be quick but his words were still lost. Over his shoulder Keith could see Jack and his men, tailing the party but rightly assessing it was too risky to rush them without somebody getting seriously hurt or killed. Nick kept glancing over his shoulder at Jack and this meant his gaze swept right over Keith. He had to be so careful, surprise was his only hope. Keith wondered whether Jack had seen him; he suspected not. He crept on, moving just a few feet at a time, ducking between one parked car and the next, judging as best he could the point at which the three of them would enter the car park. By the time they did so Keith was no more than ten metres from them, Nick's back firmly towards him. It was now or never.

Keith launched himself with all the speed of the former cross-country champion circa 1969 and the ferocity and sense of purpose inspired by terror for his son. He hurled himself straight at Nick Lawson. He might have had surprise on his side but what he met was a barrel of a man, a good six inches taller than him and thirty years younger. For a moment it looked as if Lawson would shake off the attack but then both men crashed to the ground. Keith rolled away and was on his feet first but Nick still had the gun. Keith ran towards him, Nick fired and Keith's leg buckled under him. Nick, too, was on his feet now. Keith closed his eyes; the pain ripped through him; he braced himself for the second bullet which would surely kill him. There was a thump and a grunt and Keith opened his eyes in time to see Will felling Nick with a series of body blows coming like pistons. By the time Jack Curnow and his men arrived seconds later, Will was standing over a semi-conscious Nick Lawson, his gun trained on him. Jack's boss lay on the ground with his head in Mrs Paradise's lap, blood pumping at an alarming rate from a wound in his thigh.

'Stop Dad's bleeding,' Will shouted at Jack.

'Give me your tie,' Jack said to the nearest constable. Moments later he had a tourniquet fixed and the blood was slowing. Keith seemed to be drifting in and out of consciousness. 'We'll have you in an ambulance in a tick, boss, there's one on its way.'

Keith smiled. 'Is everybody alright?'

Jack nodded, 'Fine, everything's fine.'

'Jack – Lawson, could you have a look at his hands?'

Jack bent over Nick and examined his hands, now securely handcuffed.

'Recent scarring on the fingertips,' he said with a grin.

'He got that from the chip pan,' Will explained. 'It exploded on him.'

'Did you see that or is it what he told you?' Jack asked.

Will considered the question. 'Well, he told me afterwards, I never saw it actually happen.'

'And this would be about three weeks ago, would it, Will?'

Will nodded, puzzled. 'Something like that.'

Keith tried hard to focus on Felicity from his vantage point in her lap. 'Bull's eye, Mrs Paradise,' he said thickly before his eyes closed again.

Felicity was speechless, her sense of shock total. It had all happened so quickly. She had really thought they were all going to die and the sight of her poor little puppy being kicked over the cliff like so much rubbish was too much to bear.

A police car drew up. 'I need to go with Dad,' said Will to Jack.

'No, you don't,' said Jack. 'You're coming with us.'

'But –' Will began.

'No buts, you're under arrest, there's a lot of sorting out to do, Will. I'll telephone your mother and she can meet the ambulance at Treliske.'

'Under arrest – Jack, you have to believe I wasn't involved in the arson attacks.'

'I said arrested, not charged, you're a policeman's son, you must know the difference. Now, come on.' Jack indicated towards the police car. 'The constable here will read you your rights.'

The ambulance arrived and a semi-conscious Keith was bundled into it. 'Are you his wife?' a paramedic asked. 'Do you want to come, too?'

Felicity shook her head. 'No, his wife will meet you at the hospital.'

The doors slammed and away they went. Officers were already cordoning off the scene, and Jack was issuing instructions. Nick Lawson was being ushered into a second police car. Felicity stood forlornly, alone. Having been at the centre of the drama, now she was suddenly useless. She knew she must go and look for the body of her puppy – the thought filled her with such misery that tears began pouring down her face. A crowd was gathering, staring at her but she didn't care – nothing seemed to matter.

'Mrs Paradise.' A young constable was striding across the Island; in his arms he carried something small and hairy.

'Poor Harvey!' She hurried towards him but as she neared the officer she saw that he was smiling.

'I've something you mislaid earlier,' said the young constable. 'He's alive and doesn't seem too badly hurt.' The small bundle of fur was placed in her arms, a warm lick on her cheek where her tears were freely flowing.

'How did he survive?' she asked the constable.

'He didn't fall all the way down the cliff, he landed on a patch of grass only a few feet down the slope. A lucky little chap, charmed you could say. If he had landed on a rock that would have been it.'

'I'll take him straight around to the vet,' said Felicity.

'I'd do that.'

The vet was encouraging. 'I can't see any breakages, he might have cracked something but if he had, he should be yelping. He's obviously shocked and he's going to be very bruised tomorrow.' The vet fixed her with a quizzical look over the top of his half-moon glasses. 'So, my nurse tells me you were part of the shoot out on the Island?'

'You've heard about it?' Felicity said.

'It's all over town, it's not like St Ives, it sounded more like the Wild West. Are you alright?'

'I'm fine,' said Felicity.

'Do you think you ought to take yourself off to the doctor for a check-up?'

'Absolutely not, I need to go home and look after this one and have a cup of tea.'

'You look very pale,' the vet persisted.

'I'm fine, honestly. I have a daughter in Hayle, I can always telephone her.'

'Nasty things, guns,' the vet said to Felicity's departing back.

Jericho Cottage seemed a haven after the events of the morning. Felicity glanced at her watch; it was only ten past twelve. She had been away from home for only three hours, yet it seemed like years. She gave Harvey a little dish of minced chicken which disappeared in a trice.

'I don't think you're too injured,' she said.

He wagged his tail and then staggered into his basket. Within moments the doorbell rang. It was Annie. Felicity took one look at her, threw her arms around her neck and burst into tears.

'This is not like you, my girl,' Annie said later when order had been restored with a cup of tea. The two women were sitting on the balcony looking over a deceptively tranquil St Ives.

'How did you hear about it?' Felicity asked.

'It's the talk of the town,' she said. 'Your Inspector's been shot, I gather – is he alright?'

'I don't know,' said Felicity. 'I thought I'd ring the hospital in a moment. It was a leg wound but he lost a lot of blood.'

'Saved you and his son by all accounts.'

'Yes he did,' said Felicity, 'and I did absolutely nothing, I just stood there.'

'What on earth did you think you were supposed

to do, silly girl! You're in shock, everything will settle down shortly.'

'It was the puppy, it was the way he just kicked him over the cliff, like, like he was nothing.'

'He looks fine to me now.'

'Being so young he bounced, according to the vet,' Felicity managed a smile. 'I'm just so worried about Keith.'

'Then ring the hospital,' Annie urged.

Felicity returned moments later, smiling. 'He's out of the operating theatre. It was only a flesh wound, the bullet didn't reach the bone. He's regained consciousness apparently and his wife is with him – all is well.'

'There you are,' said Annie. 'You can relax now – the puppy is safe, the Chief Inspector is safe and you're safe. What's going to happen to his boy? I gather he's involved in these arson attacks.'

'I don't know,' said Felicity, truthfully, anxious to say as little as possible. 'I don't know what's going to happen now.'

After Annie had gone, Felicity felt an overwhelming sense of exhaustion. Picking up her puppy she went downstairs and crawled into bed with him.

'This could be misinterpreted as establishing bad habits,' she said to Harvey, 'so you need to understand this is a one-off because we've had a difficult day.'

Harvey met her with a warm brown stare. It was this that had attracted her to him, she realised. Most dogs avoided eye contact but not Harvey – he stared at her knowingly. This cuddle in bed was the first of many, he knew that. Within seconds of her head touching the pillow Felicity went into a deep sleep.

She woke, confused and disorientated, to see someone standing at the end of the bed. 'What, who?' she began.

'It's alright Mum, it's only me and Minty,' said Mel.

'What are you doing here and what time is it and …' Suddenly the events of the morning flashed back into her mind and tears began streaming down her face, as she struggled into a sitting position.

'Oh, Mum.' Mel sat on the edge of the bed, baby in one arm, her hand clasping Felicity's with the other. 'Annie didn't think you were alright and you're not, are you?'

'I am really,' said Felicity. 'It was all just such a shock. I just took Harvey for a walk, I thought it was going to be …' her voice trailed away. 'What time is it, Mel?'

'It's four o'clock in the afternoon. Minty and I have come to collect you, well you both,' said Mel, smiling at Harvey. 'I gather Harvey has had quite an eventful day, too.' Harvey yawned a luxurious yawn, exposing a small pink tongue. 'Though I think you may have started something you're going to regret,' said Mel, eyeing the small figure tucked up in the duvet.

'I know, I'm hopeless, but we'd had such a

horrible morning.' Felicity agreed.

'Minty and I are here because we've all decided you should stay the night with us,' Mel said firmly.

'I'm fine,' Felicity began.

'Seriously, Mum.'

The thought of being alone and going over and over in her mind the events of the day suddenly did not seem a very attractive prospect.

'Alright,' she said, 'we give in. Give me ten minutes, I'll have a quick shower and then I'll be ready. Hello Minty.' Felicity struggled out of bed and smiled at her granddaughter. She was rewarded with a splendid toothless grin in return.

By half past five, puppy fed and watered, Felicity was sitting in one of Mel's garden chairs accepting a large glass of Pinot Grigio supplied by Martin.

'It's too early,' said Felicity. 'I never drink before six.'

'Exceptional circumstances,' said Martin, 'I'm going to join you. In France it would be six-thirty.'

'Fair enough,' said Felicity, accepting the glass gratefully.

'You're still worried,' said Martin, clinking glasses with her. Mel was bathing the baby and the two of them were alone in the sitting room.

'I'm worrying about Keith,' Felicity admitted. 'I know he's alright, I rang the hospital, but it's his son. I don't know what it would do to him if his boy was involved in the arson attacks. Jack, that's Keith's sergeant, arrested him.'

'Do you think he is, or was involved?' Martin asked.

'No, I don't,' Felicity said, 'I don't know why I say that, but it's just he seems such a decent chap. He was so kind to me when we were on the Island when Nick was brandishing the gun at us, trying to make us hurry. He took my hand and helped me, said reassuring stuff. He must have been as scared as I was but he didn't show it.'

'Army training, I suppose.' said Martin. 'Cool under fire and all that. Do you want to watch the six o'clock news? I presume it will be all over Spotlight.'

'No,' said Felicity, 'I couldn't bear it. I just want to know what's happened to Will, for Keith's sake.'

'I've an idea,' said Martin. 'I bet Arthur O'Sullivan could find out what's happened. Do you want me to ask Mel to ring him or would you like to ring him yourself?'

Felicity shook her head. 'I can't cope with Arthur tonight but that's a good idea. Do you think Mel would?'

'I'll go and see if I can take over Minty's ablutions. There is going to be no peace for you tonight until you know what's happened to Keith's boy, I can see that.'

When Mel entered the sitting room a few minutes later, she was smiling but there was a cloud hovering behind the smile. Felicity read it immediately. It was Mel's good news, bad news face. She remembered it from Mel's childhood – she had achieved eighty-one per cent in such and such an exam but had come second not first in the class and was therefore very angry with herself. She had that look now.

'What is it?' Felicity asked.

'I spoke to Arthur. The news is good, Nick Lawson is being kept in overnight and is likely to be charged tomorrow morning and refused bail. Will Penrose has been released without charge.'

'Oh, thank goodness for that.' For a moment Felicity was entirely caught up in her sense of relief, then she gave Mel a quizzical look. 'There's something else you're not telling me.'

'Not really, nothing that can't wait, it's all good, Mum.'

'Don't patronise me,' said Felicity, with a smile. 'Come on, out with it, whatever it is.'

'You won't like it.' said Mel.

'After the day I've had, it would take a lot to upset me,' said Felicity.

'This might,' Mel paused. 'Arthur O'Sullivan, my boss.'

'I know the one,' said Felicity.

'He's going to defend Nick Lawson.'

15

'Are you sure you should be coming home, Dad?' Will asked. Keith was struggling down the hospital corridor on his crutches, Will walking solicitously by his side. 'It's only twenty-four hours, surely you should give yourself another day.'

'Hospitals are very bad for your health,' Keith grumbled. 'Stop fussing, you sound like your mother.'

'She's made up a bed for you on the sofa in the sitting room so you can put your leg up and have some company.'

'Oh God,' said Keith. 'Like some bloody invalid.'

'Dad!'

'Sorry, sorry,' said Keith. What he wasn't telling his son, or indeed anybody else, was that it wasn't just his leg that hurt. It felt like every muscle in his body had been strained, every bone bruised and he was deeply angry with himself for feeling so fragile. Just a few years back, taking a tumble, fighting off a villain, would have had very little impact on him. Now he felt like an old man.

Will clearly sensed something of his father's feelings. When they reached the hospital reception, he told Keith to wait while he fetched the car. Keith didn't argue, collapsing on a chair while he waited for his son. Despite his anger with himself at his increasing frailty, the relief he felt that Will had not been charged with anything at all was enormous. Jack Curnow had visited him in hospital earlier in the day and confirmed that Will was completely in the clear; he had genuinely had no idea that Nick Lawson was the arsonist. The expression 'weak with relief' came into Keith's mind. That was exactly how he felt. The tension of wondering if his son was involved had flowed out of him like his lost blood, leaving him exhausted. Keith's own car drew to a halt outside the hospital main entrance, Will opened the door for his father and stowed his crutches on the back seat.

'What time are we expected at home?' Keith asked.

Will glanced at his watch as they drove out of the hospital entrance heading towards Truro.

'I told Mum about three.'

'Good,' said Keith, 'then we've got time to stop at a pub somewhere on the way home.'

'Should you Dad, what sort of medication are you on?'

'It's not the demon drink I'm after,' said Keith, 'it's just I'd like the chance to have a chat with you before we get home.' They lapsed into silence. Keith still felt very wary of his son. This kind, apparently solicitous young man was a great contrast to the angry drunk of just a week ago. He needed sane answers and for once he did not long to stay away from family confrontation.

They stopped at the Globe Inn in Truro, Keith extracting himself painfully from the car. Will settled him in a dark corner and ordered a pint for himself and a glass of red wine for his father.

'Well,' said Keith, when they were settled. 'Here's to survival, for both of us.' They drank in silence for a moment.

'You saved us, Dad. I think he would have shot one or both of us, he was completely out of his mind.'

'You'd have thought of something,' Keith said, 'you're a resourceful lad.'

'I rather doubt it. Anyway, thanks!'

'My pleasure,' said Keith, smiling properly for the first time. 'And Jack tells me you're in the clear.'

'Yes,' said Will, 'but I feel a bit of an idiot, not to have realised what he was up to. The thing is he is such a complex person and he was a good mate. It kind of clouds your judgement when someone saves your life.' He smiled slightly. 'People seem to be making a habit of doing that. I hope I'm worth it.'

'The business in Afghanistan,' Keith said, 'I just don't understand why you let Lawson lead you into that mess.'

'Because I was out of my depth,' Will burst out. 'I was an officer, I had free will. Instead of standing up to him and saying the raid was wrong and we weren't authorised to do it, I simply went along with it. I admired him too, you see, sort of looked up to him, wanted to be like him, I suppose.'

'And why did you?' Keith asked.

'I didn't really fit into Army life until Nick and I become friends. I suppose I was weak, the Army was right to send me packing, I'm just not officer material. I suppose I admired him because he was a good soldier and I felt sorry for him because of his childhood.'

'He told you about the accident in which his siblings were killed?'

'Yes,' said Will. 'He was only a baby so he remembers nothing of course, but he certainly knows about the consequences of the break-up of the family. His mother was off her head most of the time and his father just withdrew into himself and made no effort at all to see his son – in fact Nick was made to feel he wasn't welcome.'

'Shortly before Tom Lawson died, Nick did see his father,' Keith said.

'Yes,' said Will, 'he saw him a couple of times.'

'And was it because of this that Tom Lawson killed himself?' Keith asked. 'What's the general opinion, do you know?'

'Jack didn't interview me, of course, but when I was released without charge, we had a long chat about everything. Nick has admitted his meetings with his father were not happy occasions and that the old man didn't seem to like his long-lost son. Jack thinks Tom realised what Nick was up to. He believes Tom

Lawson killed himself because those three little Belcher children died. He saw that the tragedy which had destroyed his family, through Nick's madness, had also caused the death of three more innocent children. He just couldn't cope with it, or Nick himself, I suspect.'

'From what I understand Tom had probably wanted to kill himself for years. I can quite see that the attack on the Belcher house was the final straw, if he thought his son had caused it. Tell me, Will, you must have been aware of Nick's declining mental state?' Keith asked.

'Oh yes,' said Will, 'and I didn't know what to do about it. We'd been through such a lot together, Dad – Iraq, Afghanistan and its subsequent fall-out, being drummed out of the Army, the shame of losing our careers and then of course the underlying fact that he did save my life without question. I keep thinking ...' Will broke off for a moment and took a sip of his pint. He gazed out of the window avoiding his father's eyes.

'You keep thinking what?' Keith asked.

'I keep thinking if I'd realised what Nick was up to then maybe those Belcher children needn't have died. If I had just been more alert ... It just never occurred to me to link the two. I knew he was nuts, but not that nuts.'

'You can't put that one on yourself, Will,' Keith said. 'We should have picked up the Culdrose helicopter crash on the Lizard, but I wasn't looking for the right thing. I was looking for an incident where someone could have thought Culdrose had let them down. Also, we weren't looking back far enough. With the benefit of hindsight, I presume you now recognise that after the Belcher fire, Lawson's behaviour rapidly deteriorated.'

'Yes,' Will agreed. 'Basically he was pissed all the time, morning till night, and very aggressive. It must have been terrible to live with the consequences of what he'd done in the light of what had happened in Afghanistan. It was history repeating itself – no wonder he went off his head.'

'Yes,' Keith agreed. 'And you are aware, I assume, that he set fire to the wrong house. He was trying to burn down the cottage of a travel writer called Philip Ferguson, but in the dark he confused the two cottages. He certainly never meant to harm those children. I don't think he meant to harm anyone. He seems deliberately to have chosen cottages where people were away. I think once he'd done the first cottage, he found it exhilarating, almost a relief from his warped pent-up feelings. Each time he set fire to a cottage, he felt he was paying back for what had happened to his family and then, of course, it all went pear-shaped when he picked the wrong cottage. If anyone should be slaying themselves for what happened to the Belcher children, it's me. I should have found him sooner but at the time we just had nothing to go on. One thing which still puzzles me is how he got his information. I must ask Jack about that.'

'I know,' said Will, quietly.

'You know? How did he do it then, Will?'

'He had this lady friend in St Ives. An older woman, married. Nick always goes for the same type – older than him with commitments. We used to tease him about it in the regiment. I think he felt safe with them – no demands, no requirement to become seriously involved.' Will took a sip of his beer. 'Anyway, this woman, Evie her name is, has a small business which handles changeovers – she and her team clean and maintain holiday lets. Nick was always buzzing off to see her. It was how they managed their relationship – you know,' Will looked embarrassed, 'an empty cottage needing a clean meant they had somewhere to …'

'I get the picture,' said Keith, smiling at his son's discomfiture.

'Anyway, I guess it's what you call pillow talk. Unintentionally, Evie told Nick all about the people in the cottages she cleaned.'

'Christ, why didn't we pick up the connection? Does Jack know this?' Keith had turned a dangerous shade of puce.

'Calm down, Dad. Yes, Jack knows and Evie has been interviewed. You wouldn't have picked up the connection because Evie's business is nothing formal – no smart van, or business name. It's just a group of mainly married women with children who work together to cover a number of cottages and earn a bit of cash.'

'All the same, damn it.' Keith slumped back in his seat.

The two men drank in silence for a moment. 'What are you going to do now, Will?' Keith asked, seeming anxious to change the subject from the source of so much missed opportunity.

'There's a boat-building course in Falmouth, I've been thinking about it for a few weeks. You know I've always loved DT and messing about in boats. It seems to bring the whole thing together. I was wondering if it would be possible to come and live back at home while I do the course? It's for a year, and then if I pass all the right exams, I can get an apprenticeship and be able to afford a place of my own.'

'Have you discussed it with your mother?'

'Yes, last night when I got back from the Station. I think she was so relieved I hadn't been charged, she'd have agreed to anything. Are you OK with it?'

'I don't know,' said Keith. He took a sip of his wine and looked out of the window, apparently lost in thought.

'What do you mean?' Will demanded. The aggression was back.

'If you were still a boy, I would have no hesitation in saying yes, Will, but you're a grown man. You've put your mother through hell in the last few weeks with your drinking and your anger. She shouldn't, mustn't have to cope with that again.'

'She's happy to have me.'

'Oh, grow up, Will, for God's sake. She's your

mother. If you had been responsible for those arson attacks instead of Lawson, she would still have loved you, still worried herself sick about you. She'll agree to anything, but as far as I'm concerned, if you want to come back home, then I need guarantees.'

'Great, so when I need a helping hand, as usual my father doesn't give it. No change there.'

Keith fought his rising temper. 'You can come back home on probation, provided you find some other outlet for your anger other than using your parents as a punch bag, provided you go for counselling and cut down the drinking.'

'You're treating me like a kid. What sort of outlet for my anger do you have in mind?'

Keith eyed him. 'Well once I'm fit again, we could pay squash a couple of times a week.'

'Oh, please, and how am I supposed to dispose of the other ninety-nine per cent of my pent-up anger?'

There was a silence while the two men stared at one another. Suddenly from nowhere a bubble of laughter escaped from Keith, and in seconds they were both drowned in it. 'Maybe we could add a round or two of table tennis,' Keith suggested, wiping his eyes.

Eventually they sobered. 'I'll try,' said Will. 'My life is just such a mess; I should never have gone into the Army.'

'I never understood why you did,' said Keith, 'I never felt it was right for you.'

'You didn't say at the time,' said Will, accusingly.

'I tried to, but probably I didn't try hard enough.'

'I think I wanted to do one better than you,' said Will, 'very childish when I think about it now. In my mixed-up teenage eyes, you were just a policeman coping with the odd bit of domestic violence and the occasional robbery. I wanted to do things on the world stage rather than within the confines of Cornwall. Pathetic really but I think it's fairly standard stuff to want to outshine one's father.'

'I suppose,' said Keith. 'I'm sorry, I should have realised.'

'Let's change the subject, Dad,' Will said. 'I'm fed up with talking about me and I do have a couple of questions.'

'What more?' Keith managed a smile.

'What will happen to Nick now?'

'I don't know,' Keith said. 'It depends on how his mental state is assessed. He certainly won't be charged with murder of the Belcher children but possibly manslaughter. Arson, of course, is a serious offence because it is both premeditated and is so potentially lethal. So much depends on how much his mental state is taken into account but it may well be that he ends up receiving treatment rather than punishment. Who knows, he may come through it, learn to live with what happened.'

'But on top of what happened in Afghanistan, Dad, he's got five deaths on his hands.'

'Five?' Keith said.

'The three Belcher children and their mother

201

and his own father. I don't see how anyone survives that.'

'And the second question?' Keith asked, wanting to move on from the bleakness of Nick Lawson's future.

'This Mrs Paradise,' Will said, grinning. 'You're not having a thing with her, are you Dad?'

Keith smiled. 'No, of course I'm not, I'm married to your mother, remember.'

'It's just, well, I wouldn't blame you, Dad. She's a very attractive woman and you seem so very fond of one another. When you were shot, she was in a complete state. There you were, lying with your head in her lap – it seemed like you knew each other so well, cared about each other so much. It's none of my business, I know, I just ...' his voice tailed away.

Keith stared down at his empty wine glass, trying to find the right words. 'I have become very fond of Mrs Paradise over the last few years, that's true, but I would never betray the trust put in me by your mother and nor would I presume to make any overtures towards Mrs Paradise other than that of friendship. We are good friends, good pals, that's all there is to it, Will, honestly.'

'Only I wouldn't blame you, Dad. I know Mum isn't the easiest person, she can be a bit full-on. She means well but she can't be easy to live with – I see that now having lived away from home for so long.'

'Enough,' said Keith, 'I won't hear you say a word against your mother. She has put up with me for all these years – the woman is a saint.'

'That's true,' said Will, smiling. 'You're not a bad old sod, Dad, are you?'

'I'll take that as a compliment,' said Keith.

While Keith and his son were sitting in the Globe, Felicity and Harvey had returned home. Felicity was sitting on her balcony with a cup of tea, drinking in the view of St Ives Bay. She had rung the hospital earlier to hear that Keith had been discharged. She knew that she should feel relaxed but instead she felt oddly strung-up. Out of deference to her ordeal, Jack Curnow had come to Mel's house earlier that morning to take a statement, to save Felicity having to go to the police station. Reliving the whole ordeal had not been pleasant but Jack had been kind and gentle.

At the end of the interview they chatted for a few minutes. 'I knew he was up to something,' Jack said, smiling. 'His radio was switched off and his mobile. I knew he was in town and I suspected he was close but he took me by surprise as much as Lawson. I don't know what we'd have done without him, though. Me and my men couldn't have jumped Lawson, not without putting you in terrible danger. Quite the hero, our Chief Inspector.'

'Yes,' said Felicity, 'yes he is.'

That was what felt wrong, Felicity thought. Keith had saved her and he was the only person who could now make her feel better. The phone rang, making her jump. She got up reluctantly to answer it in the kitchen.

'Felicity, it's Arthur O'Sullivan here, I gather you've been in the wars.'

'I haven't, not really,' said Felicity, 'but Harvey has.'

'Harvey?'

'My puppy,' she said.

Arthur was clearly unmoved. 'I was wondering if you'd like to have dinner with me tonight, to cheer you up after your ordeal?'

'No thanks,' said Felicity.

'A drink then?'

'I've only just come home; I stayed with Mel last night. I need to sort myself out, tidy up, touch base. I feel a bit disorientated.'

'What about later then?'

She was about to decline when the temptation to tell Arthur O'Sullivan what she thought of him was suddenly overwhelming. 'Alright,' she said. 'Nine at the Sloop; will that be too late for you?'

'Not at all, I'll be there,' he replied.

He was already waiting for her when she arrived spot on time. He had a bottle of champagne in an ice bucket and two glasses.

'I felt a little celebration was in order.' She declined to make any comment and followed him stiffly to a corner table. He poured two glasses and handed one to her. 'To survival,' he said.

Felicity took a sip without replying, then could contain herself no longer. 'So the champagne would suggest you are pleased I survived,' she said.

'Of course, my darling girl,' said Arthur, gallantly.

'I'm not your darling girl and if you're so pleased I have survived, how come you're going to defend the man who could have killed me?'

'Felicity, my dear, this is not worthy of you, a lawyer's wife. The two things are totally unrelated. I'm deeply fond of you and extremely pleased that you came through what must have been an horrendous experience unscathed – thanks, I understand, in no small way to your Inspector friend. My representing Lawson is a completely separate professional matter – you of all people must surely see that.'

'No, I don't,' said Felicity.

'Then I am afraid to say you are being completely unreasonable. I'm sure your husband often took cases about which you did not approve.'

'Only the once,' said Felicity, in a small voice, 'and it killed him.'

'That sounds like a threat,' said Arthur, only half-joking.

'No it's not a threat, just a fact.'

'Do you want to tell me about it?' Arthur asked.

'No, not really.' She put down her glass. 'Nor do I really want this champagne, nor do I want to drink it with you. I'm sorry Arthur, there is of course absolutely no reason at all why you shouldn't take the Lawson case. I imagine it will be quite a high-profile case and an interesting one, too – the balance of his mind and all that – but I thought he was going to kill us, Arthur. I think if he had reached the car he might have done so. You said the other night that you thought our relationship had a long-term future. If you meant what you said I do not understand how you feel it appropriate to represent Nick Lawson. If things were the other way round, if you were the victim and I the lawyer, there is no way I would have been prepared to represent him.'

'I bet your husband would have done,' Arthur said.

'I can't speak for Charlie,' said Felicity. 'I can only say that if he had, I would have been very disappointed with him. Now, if you'll excuse me.'

'You're going?' Arthur sounded surprised.

Felicity stood up and Arthur did, too. 'Yes,' she said. 'We won't be seeing each other again but please don't take this out on Mel. She's a good girl and a talented one – in my view you are lucky to have her.'

'I agree,' said Arthur, 'you must think I'm extremely petty-minded if you imagine I would react in such a way.'

'I don't know what you are, Arthur, that's the trouble,' said Felicity and with that she turned her back and walked steadily out of the pub.

Once outside she turned left and began walking along the Wharf towards the Pier, taking childish satisfaction from the fact that Arthur O'Sullivan would look rather stupid drinking a bottle of champagne on his own. She walked quickly breathing in the warm, salty air. It was a wonderful night, star-studded and turning left by the Pier, she headed towards the museum and slowed her pace. She wondered if she was right about Charlie. Would he have turned down the opportunity of such a high-profile lucrative case out of sensitivity towards his wife? She was no longer sure. The events surrounding Charlie's death had left her confused. Was he really the man she had always imagined she'd been married to or, in fact, was he a charming stranger with his dark secrets? Looking back, knowing how consistently over the years he had lied to her, it was hard to identify the real man. She walked gingerly down the steps to Porthgwidden Car Park, holding the handrail as she was still stiff. She walked across the car park and stopped to gaze down at Porthgwidden beach, now deserted, the lights from the café creating shadows across the sand. She looked up and there, ahead of her, was the Island, the outline of the chapel clearly visible against the darkening sky. She shuddered; she was not ready for the Island yet, she'd go back home through town.

At the sound of her key turning in the lock, there was excited yelping from within and Harvey half-bounded, half-fell down the stairs into her arms. She remembered what Arthur had said about coming home to an empty house – well, not any more. Who needed a man in one's life when one could enjoy the

16

It was nearly ten days after the arrest of Nicholas Lawson when Keith and Felicity finally met again. Keith was still not able to drive and they arranged to meet at the Heron at Malpas, Keith being dropped off by Jack Curnow and Felicity promising to return him to Truro after lunch. Jack smiled at Felicity as he helped his boss up the steps to the terrace where Felicity was waiting.

'I'm not sure it's safe to leave you two together,' he said. 'You always seem to run into trouble. Can you be trusted to have a quiet and uneventful lunch?'

'Absolutely,' Felicity agreed. 'I'll take great care of him, I promise.'

'Do please try,' said Jack, as he headed back to the car.

Keith eased himself into a seat. Felicity had ordered a bottle of wine. Being a Monday there were few people around. The Fal stretched out below them; a heron flapped across the creek. It was a beautiful tranquil scene.

'Well,' said Keith.

'Well, yourself,' said Felicity. 'How are you feeling?'

'OK, stiff and old, but then that's only appropriate.' Keith smiled and began pouring the wine. 'And you?'

'Stiff and old,' Felicity agreed, 'and very grateful. Thanks, Keith.'

'It wasn't a good situation, was it?'

'It was terrifying,' said Felicity. 'God knows how you must have felt, seeing your son at the point of a gun. I can't even begin to imagine,' she hesitated. 'It's not often that words fail me.'

Keith smiled at her. 'I've noticed, and yes, it was desperate seeing my son and my very good friend in such danger.' He leant across and put a hand on hers for a moment. At the gesture, Felicity felt sudden tears come into her eyes. She looked away hurriedly and a movement by her feet gave her the opportunity of a diversion. She leant down and scooped up Harvey.

'Well, this young man seems to have survived the ordeal better than either of us.'

'The advantage of having youth on his side.' Keith removed his hand from hers and took the puppy onto his lap. 'You forget, don't you, that puppy smell, it's like new babies.'

'He's a good chap,' said Felicity, 'and he's going to be an excellent companion, which is good as I've given up on men completely.'

'Really?' Keith asked.

Suddenly Felicity wasn't ready to talk about herself.

'How's Will?' she asked hurriedly.

Always tuned to her feelings, Keith took the bait. 'He's fine, dreading the trial of course, knowing that he'll have to testify against Lawson but he also recognises that it has to be done.' He hesitated. 'He's damaged, damaged by his relationship with Lawson but I think more so from his relationship with the Army. I think the theatre of war is at the moment particularly brutalising for the young men in the Army. It's so complicated, they're supposed to be peacekeepers but most of the time they're in mortal danger, particularly in Afghanistan. There is no clear idea who the enemy is and so often civilians are caught up in the conflict – it is a far cry from traditional battle lines.'

'I'm glad my boy, James, has never had to experience that. Mind you,' Felicity smiled, 'he'd be absolutely hopeless, he's a complete boffin.'

'I think Will had to force himself to cope with Army life, which is why, of course, he made such a bad decision and latched onto Lawson, for support as much as anything else. Lawson was a much stronger, more charismatic figure than Will, and in many respects an ideal soldier.'

'And I suppose being a parent, you blame yourself for him being in the Army at all?'

Keith smiled. 'What a perceptive woman you

are, Mrs Paradise. Yes, of course I blame myself and of course I'm right to do so. Will more or less admits that he went into the Army to outdo me. I was keeping the peace in West Cornwall, he wanted to do it on a global scale. He needed to do better.'

'So why was that?'

'Presumably because I have not been able to make him confident enough of himself in his own right.'

'In the end,' said Felicity, 'we can only do our best and whatever our shortcomings we can't keep beating ourselves up about it. He grew up in a loving family; if he chose to have a complex about his successful father and to let that feeling influence his choice of career, well that was a bad mistake which Will Penrose made, not you.'

'Oh, that it was that easy.'

'I agree,' said Felicity. 'My two are so different and their extremes of character couldn't be more diverse, but of course I blame myself for both Mel's bossiness and James's shyness – all my fault.'

'Naturally,' said Keith. He put the puppy down on the floor. 'Shall I go and order us some food?'

'I'll do it,' said Felicity, 'you sit tight. What would you like?'

They chose from the menu and Felicity went into the bar to place their order. When she returned Keith was leaning back against the wall of the pub, eyes closed, relaxed in the sunshine. She couldn't ever remember catching him off guard before and smiled fondly at him. Sensing her gaze he opened his eyes.

'Sorry, it's just so relaxing here.'

'How long are you off work?' She asked, sitting down beside him.

'Officially, another couple of weeks but I'll have cabin fever long before then. I expect I'll go back at the end of next week, I'm driving Barbara mad already.'

'What on earth is going to happen to you when you retire?' Felicity asked.

'God knows,' said Keith. 'I'll have to find some extremely absorbing hobby or I'll go insane. It will have to be something physical, I don't want to get fat and flabby but it absolutely cannot be golf, I cannot stand the whole thing – all the silly clothes, club rules, golfing dinners – all that fuss about bashing a small ball round a field.'

'No, I can't see you propping up the bar of the golf club, not you at all. Well, that will give me some food for thought in my idle moments, finding you an occupation.'

'I'd be grateful,' said Keith. There was a pause while their food was served. Keith began picking at his lasagne with little enthusiasm.

'Not hungry?' Felicity asked.

'No, not really.'

'Do you feel alright?'

'Yes, yes fine,' he said. 'It's probably the pain killers, I certainly don't have much appetite these days.'

'You've been shot twice in the time I've known you,' said Felicity, 'that's probably more than the average Chief Inspector receives, by way of injury, in the whole of his working life – then only if he's based in some violent inner city. Here you are in tranquil Cornwall and you seem to get treated like a firing range.'

'It's the company I keep,' said Keith, smiling at her. 'I know this mad woman who's always up to her neck in trouble and it's my unfortunate job to keep her in one piece … and look what happens to me!'

'It's true,' said Felicity. 'I can't deny it.'

'What was all this about you giving up men?' He gave her a searching look.

'Oh, nothing really.'

'Would it have anything to do with Arthur O'Sullivan?'

'Yes.'

'Your friendship with him is over?'

'It is and it was a bad mistake. The man is a shallow, unprincipled idiot.'

'Aah,' said Keith, 'I did warn you.'

'Don't you dare say I told you so. I met him in the Sloop the other night and he had the appalling bad taste to have a bottle of champagne waiting for me. I nearly threw it in his face.'

'What was he celebrating?' Keith asked.

'My survival, completely airbrushing the fact that he is going to represent the man who could quite easily have killed me. He couldn't see that there was any problem with that. He said that as the wife of a lawyer I shouldn't be so naïve. Naïve, after what I went through with Charlie! I had to stamp round the whole of St Ives to calm down. At least I left him with his wretched bottle of champagne, looking a complete twit, which he is.'

'Ah,' said Keith.

'Don't gloat,' said Felicity, crossly. Her colour was high, she looked absurdly young with eyes flashing, arms gesturing with agitation.

'I don't mean to gloat,' said Keith. 'I'm just relieved.'

'You men are all the same, you're never what you seem, you say one thing and mean another, you're not to be trusted. There I was all those years married to Charlie and all the time he was deceiving me, and Arthur accuses me of being naïve just because I don't want to go out with a man who's defending the person who was brandishing a gun at me. From now on the only man in my life is going to be Harvey.'

'Not me?' Keith asked.

Felicity stopped her ranting and looked into Keith's face; she saw deep hurt there. It surprised her and made her heart skip a beat.

'You don't count,' she said, in what she thought was a reassuring voice. The hurt seemed to deepen, hanging in the air between them.

'Not count?' he said, his voice bleak.

She put her hand on his arm. 'Oh, Keith, I mean that in a good way, not a bad way.'

As Felicity herself had done earlier, he turned from her and gazed out across the creek as if studying something very interesting there. 'Will asked me about you, about us.'

'What did he say?' Felicity asked.

'He asked whether we were having an affair, he said he wouldn't mind, he'd understand.' Keith managed to meet her eye again. 'He said you're a cracker or words to that effect, and he's right, of course.'

'How very gallant of him, of you both,' said Felicity, trying to make light of the moment.

'I told him that of course I wasn't and that I could never be unfaithful to his mother.' Keith searched her face for understanding. 'Which is true.'

'I know,' said Felicity, gently.

'But I do care about you very deeply,' said Keith. 'You're very special, but even if you'd have me, it wouldn't be right – you deserve better than secondhand goods.' The atmosphere between them crackled with tension. 'Will said that you were very upset when I was shot.'

'Of course I was, you silly old idiot.' They smiled at one another, relieved. Some sort of hurdle seemed to have been overcome.

'Is it possible for an unrelated man and woman of comparable age to love one another without, well you know, a full-on relationship?' Keith asked.

'Yes,' said Felicity, 'we're living proof.'

'It's complicated though,' said Keith. 'I was

jealous of Arthur, no doubt about it.'

'Well you needn't be jealous any more,' said Felicity. 'I have taken a vow of celibacy. I'll rephrase what I said earlier; there are in fact two men in my life, you and Harvey. Is that any better?'

'Much better,' said Keith. 'I love you, Mrs Paradise.'

'I love you too, Chief Inspector Penrose. Now drink up and I'll take you home before we start blubbing into our wine.'

'That wouldn't be our style,' Keith said.

'No, it certainly wouldn't,' Felicity replied, briskly.